THE CASE OF
THOMAS N.

THE CASE OF THOMAS N.

A novel by
John David Morley

THE ATLANTIC MONTHLY PRESS
New York

FIRST EDITION

Library of Congress Cataloging-in-Publication Data

Morley, John David, 1948–
The case of Thomas N.

I. Title.
PR6063.07446C3 1987 813'.54   87-1066
ISBN 0-87113-152-8

Printed in the United States of America

Designed by Laura Hough

For Armgard

THE CASE OF
THOMAS N.

Early one morning in June a destitute boy was found by a police officer sitting on a bench by the river. The boy was in a confused state of mind and his replies to the policeman's questions were barely coherent. As he was obviously unable to give any account of himself, or what he was doing there, the officer asked the boy to accompany him back to the station. The boy got up and followed him without a word. He seemed indifferent to what happened to him.

The police questioned him for over an hour without success. Beyond his first name, which he gave as Thomas, he was not able to tell them anything about himself at all, where he came from, who his parents were, not even how old he was. He couldn't say where he had been the day before, how he came to be sitting by the river, or where he had been intending to go from there.

The police were mystified. They didn't have the impression the boy was lying and so far as they could tell he seemed to be of normal intelligence. Yet it was apparent that the business of being questioned caused him a certain discomfort; not the questions as such but the fact that he was being asked any questions at all. He seemed just as puzzled by their asking him so many questions as they were by his inability to answer them.

The boy was shabbily dressed and carried a battered suitcase. He couldn't say for sure what was in it, but he thought "probably clothes and some belongings." He was asked to open it and have a look, as they might perhaps find something which

———

would help them further. Reluctantly he handed the case over. However, when the police tried to open it they found it was locked. Where had he put the key?

This question had a very startling effect on the boy. He leaped to his feet and began turning out his pockets in an agitated manner. He had kept the key here, he said, unbuttoning his shirt, on a string around his neck, but it was no longer there. It wasn't in his pockets either. He'd lost the key! Lost it! He repeated this anxiously over and over again. The police tried to calm him down. It didn't matter if he could not find the key, they said, since they would be able to open the case anyhow. But these attempts to reassure him made no difference. The key seemed to have an importance for the boy out of all proportion to the fact that its only purpose was to unlock the case.

Eventually the case was opened and the police began to examine its contents. Jacket, trousers, socks, underwear. The articles were piled on the bench beside the suitcase one by one. They made a note of the makers' names and, in one case, a laundry mark. Everything was in a very bad state of repair; buttons were missing, there were holes in the socks. Apart from that, the clothes stank. On top of them lay a pile of sandwiches, at least several days old, in a broken paper bag. There was another smell too, almost palpable: the dense, musty odor of clothes that have lain unused for a very long time.

Towards the bottom of the suitcase the police came across a wallet. They asked the boy to empty its contents onto the table. There was a small quantity of money in notes and coins, some of which had been withdrawn from currency a few years previously, a bus ticket and a photograph. The photograph was blurred and one corner was torn. It showed an extremely handsome woman, perhaps in her early thirties, standing against a wall and looking straight ahead, not directly into the camera but slightly to one side of it. She wore a summer frock and it appeared as if she were smiling, but this impression

---

might have been due to the strong light. It looked like a holiday snap. On the back of the photograph a word or part of a word, *gadá,* and underneath it a date, unfortunately illegible, had been stamped in bluish italics. The boy said he had no idea who the woman was, and the name *gadá* meant nothing to him.

At the bottom of the case they found a small pillow or cushion and a pair of tennis shoes. There was nothing unusual about these tennis shoes except the newspaper they were wrapped in—it was fifteen years old. When one of the police officers lifted out the newspaper a little plastic capsule that had been lying underneath it rolled free. He opened it, sniffed it and shook out a tiny quantity onto the tip of his finger. The brownish color and bitter taste of the substance suggested that it might be opium.

Saying nothing about what he had found, the officer casually placed the capsule on the table beside the other things and asked the boy to put his belongings back into the case. He packed the case in the reverse order, starting with the clothes that had lain on top and ending with the shoes and pillow which had been lying at the bottom. He replaced the capsule without giving it a second glance. The complete naturalness with which he did this made it seem likely that he had no idea what it was. Not only the reversed order but also the quite different way in which he now packed the case indicated that it might originally have been packed by someone else. Instead of folding the trousers as they had been before, he rolled them; and the sleeves of the jacket were not tucked in across the breast but folded out over the back, rather as if he were tying someone's hands. It seemed a peculiar way of doing it.

The discovery of the opium capsule supplied the starting point for the police theory about the otherwise inexplicable condition of the boy and the mysterious circumstances in which he had been found. Not surprisingly they reached the conclusion that he was at present, and most likely for some time past

---

5

had been, under the influence of opium and perhaps other narcotics as well. His total disorientation began to appear a little less strange.

Although no charges were preferred, the boy was detained at the station. In the course of the morning it was arranged for him to be seen by a doctor. He smelled so offensive, however, that before the doctor could be expected to examine him it was agreed that he ought to take a bath. His clothes were literally rotting on him, and when he could finally be persuaded to part with them they were taken out into the yard and burned.

The doctor's report was not available until the afternoon, as it took a little time for the results of the blood test the police had requested to be sent on from the laboratory. To nobody's surprise, traces of opium had been identified.

The doctor added a cautionary note. In his opinion the boy showed symptoms of disorientation not typically associated with the effects of opium or of any other drug either. There was no doubt at all that they were dealing here with a massive amnesic syndrome, but it was a delicate matter to decide where its causes might lie.

"The subject suffers from slight malnutrition, has possibly been exposed to drugs over quite a long period of time and can in consequence be expected to have led a very irregular life. While such factors may be adduced to explain his precarious balance of mind, they hardly extend to the condition of amnesia in such an extreme degree. It must be assumed that he has sustained a serious shock, of a psychological kind, or suffered some accident or illness which has impaired his brain. There is a scar at the back of the skull, perhaps dating from early childhood, but in consideration of its size, position etc. it can only have been a surface wound which would probably not have had any effect on the brain. A record of illness can be no more than

6

a conjecture. There are no outward indications of any disease the subject has had which might theoretically be associated with impairment of the brain. Though a little underfed, the subject is in a reasonably sound state of health. Accordingly it must be concluded that the causes of his condition are predominantly psychological, and he ought to be examined by a psychiatrist as soon as possible.

"For purposes of identification it should be noted that he has a small brown birthmark on the inside of his right wrist. His age can be estimated at about sixteen or seventeen."

These findings were not much help to the police. The psychiatrist to whom they were advised to refer the case was out of town and would not be available until the following morning. In the meantime what were they to do with the boy? There was no alternative but to keep him in the station that night and await the psychiatrist's verdict the next day.

Using more sophisticated techniques, two officers again interrogated the boy later that afternoon. The session continued for a couple of hours. Who are you? Where is your home? The boy must have been asked these questions at least a hundred times. At first they merely bewildered him. He didn't understand what his interrogators were talking about. It seemed he thought that what they were really interested in was how he had lost the suitcase key. He became increasingly sullen, and finally refused to answer their questions at all.

The long, dreary march through state institutions had begun. The boy was photographed and his fingerprints put on file. The photograph and a detailed description were put out for circulation with a request for any further information that might help to identify him. He was listed as a missing person. Under the heading "Subject" was typed the name Thomas, followed by a question mark, with the words "Name unknown" in brackets. In later references to the case he was known simply as Thomas N.

In the evening he was given a light supper, which he barely touched, although he had said he was hungry. He complained peevishly about the taste of the water.

One of the night duty officers showed him the cell where he was to spend the night. To his astonishment the boy asked to be locked in. Having been given instructions to make his charge feel as comfortable as was possible under the circumstances, the officer felt reluctant to do this, but the boy was so insistent that he eventually gave way.

At eight o'clock the following morning he was driven over to the clinic where it had been arranged for him to be examined by a psychiatrist. The upshot of this examination was that application should be made for him to be detained in a clinic for an initial observation period of not more than three weeks under the provisions of the mental health act. The examining psychiatrist was so intrigued by the curious nature of the case that he requested the patient's transfer to a semiprivate institution where he had his own extensive practice. He could do no more than confirm the one outstanding feature of the case: the boy had completely lost his memory.

From the very outset the case of Thomas N. was characterized by paradox. On the one hand it was perfectly clear what was wrong with him, and on the other his condition remained inexplicable.

Dr. Ormond, the psychiatrist in charge, tentatively endorsed his colleague's view that the causes of the boy's condition were not to be attributed to some physical injury. His own examination had likewise failed to reveal any marks or bruises such as might be expected if, for example, the boy had been knocked down by a car, which would have plausibly accounted for a spontaneous global amnesia. And in any case, memory disturbances associated with injury were typically of limited extent, both in respect to the period for which memories were erased and the memory functions that were affected. For some periods there would be a lot of clear memories, while for others none at all; knowledge too basic even to be regarded as such, like one's name and age, was forgotten, while an ability to solve complicated problems might remain intact. But the mind of Thomas N. appeared to be quite simply blank.

In cases of psychologic amnesia clinical observation tended to confirm that loss of memory usually involved doubt about personal identification, disorientation in time and space, misidentification of other people, lack of—or only very tenuous —subjective certainty about the reality of events the patient recalled or thought he recalled, and many other symptoms of a similar kind.

9

Despite certain parallels, the case of Thomas N. was distinguished from all these by several remarkable factors: no clinical antecedents were known, no source of information concerning the subject was available except for the subject himself, and even he recalled nothing. It made little sense to speak of disorientation at all, for the problem of Thomas N. presented itself in a solitude so absolute that no point was given by which this could have been defined.

He gave no indication of being aware of his condition. Dr. Ormond asked him the same question repeatedly:

"Do you realize you have lost your memory?"

The boy looked at him vacantly, not understanding the question. At the same time he appeared to be aware of *something*. He had something on his mind. He was uneasy, in the groping, incoherent way characteristic of loss of memory.

Dr. Ormond began to have an inkling of what it was that troubled him about the boy after he had listened to the tape recording of the interrogation which had been conducted at the police station. He compared it with recordings of his own interviews with him. They all had something in common which for a long time he was unable to put his finger on. The resemblance lay not in something the boy was saying but in something he was not saying. Thomas N. did not once use the first personal pronoun.

It was this omission of the word *I*, the most common word in the spoken language, which accounted for the peculiar impression of the boy's speech. Its mode was holophrastic, like the speech of small children, in which the deep structure contained more and even quite other information than was apparent in its surface form. The dense texture of his speech was not however a result of limited resources of syntax, as in the case of a small child, but of a fundamental lack of clarity. Simple, active, declarative sentences were conspicuous by their absence. He had a preference for impersonal constructions and for transforming sentences that ought naturally to have required himself as subject into sentences where he appeared as the object, some other person being named as the agent. Events would usually be described from a point of view other than his own.

It seemed to Dr. Ormond that there was a significant parallel between, on the one hand linguistically, statements which it was impossible to trace back to the kernel sentences from which they had presumably been transformed and, on the other hand psychologically, a state of consciousness which did not apparently have any point of origin.

He brought the matter up with a friend, who pointed out that there were languages in which the subject word was very often omitted.

"How does that work in practice?"

"The verb has no number. The subject just disappears into the verb. This has rather interesting implications. Our own view of life is strongly influenced by the fact that subjects and their predicates are morphologically distinct. Constant reiteration of the subject has the effect of keeping the agent and his action apart, perhaps of dissociating the subject from his experience of the world in a fundamental way. But when the subject is incorporated in the verb there's no such distinction. He merges quite naturally and organically with the world around him. The concept of self is differentiated according to the concept of other, without which it effectively ceases to exist. Very different, you see, from our own notion of a wholly autonomous sovereign self."

This account intrigued Dr. Ormond. He found himself contemplating the "wholly autonomous sovereign self," as his friend called it, with a sense of disconcerting unfamiliarity. Responding to one's name and being able to refer to oneself as "I" occurred so naturally that the idea of recognizing it as a capacity just did not arise.

Conceivably Thomas N. did not know who he was not

because he was unable to refer to himself or to remember his name, but because there was nothing in him to which a name might correspond. And what it corresponded to was just such a capacity, acquired only by a preposterous act of faith once it had been lost or questioned, to experience all thoughts and sensations as emanating from one source and belonging to one subject that remained continuously itself throughout time and space.

Although Thomas N. did not appear to understand that he had lost his memory, Dr. Ormond was alert to the significance of the missing suitcase key. The boy returned to the subject of the key constantly. During his stay at the clinic its function was taken over by other substitutes such as a beaker, a vase and a wastepaper basket—objects which for one reason or another had been temporarily removed from his room.

Because he was attached to these objects he seemed to feel responsible for them, and when he discovered they were missing his reaction was always the same: an extraordinary display of guilt. Altogether it seemed to be characteristic of the boy that his interest in things only became evident when they were missing.

About a week after his admission to the clinic, during lunch in the canteen, he suddenly overturned a table and began smashing whatever he could lay his hands on. The outburst subsided as abruptly as it had arisen, and he relapsed into an apathy from which nothing could stir him. For days on end he sat with his face to the wall, hardly speaking and refusing to eat. He grew weak, body and mind began to disintegrate.

Dr. Ormond's way of dealing with this behavior was to do nothing. He reasoned that so long as the boy continued to play a wholly passive part in an environment which did not require him to do otherwise there was little chance of his improving anyhow. He must make up his mind for himself whether he wanted to live. So the nurse in charge was instructed to give any help that was needed, but only if specifically requested.

Left to his own devices, the boy sat in his room doing nothing. He was still not eating anything but, as Dr. Ormond had foreseen, it was now no longer a refusal to eat, since nothing was offered for him to refuse. He had been maneuvered into making a choice, and it became his own responsibility.

On the fifth morning of his self-imposed fast it was reported that he had been along to the dining hall to eat breakfast.

Thomas N. had unpleasant eating habits. He ate noisily and in a very clumsy way. He showed a preference for liquid foods; he particularly liked soups and stews. He drank straight from the bowl or saucer, or even with a straw. Sometimes several items of cutlery, including an array of spoons, would be laid out on the table. He sucked, poured, slurped and flicked the contents of the bowl into his mouth. His use of a spoon was grotesque. He would twist and thrust it deep into his gullet. Much of what he was attempting to eat thus landed on his clothes, the table and the floor. He gave the impression of somehow wanting to abuse or punish the food, to do everything with it except put it in his mouth. When he did achieve this it seemed almost unintentional, as if he had tricked himself into eating it.

There was no accounting for his persistent comments on the taste of water. Whenever he asked for water, he complained, he would be given something else instead. It never had the taste of water. But water doesn't have any taste, they said. He insisted that it did. One explanation that occurred to Dr. Ormond was that the boy had been accustomed to drink something passed off as water in which some other substance had secretly been diluted.

The information about Thomas N. was so meager that every aspect of his behavior was monitored, without his knowledge, for whatever clues it might give, much as an animal is observed in a controlled environment. Of particular interest to his observers were the basic bodily functions, what he ate and drank, how often waste matter was discharged, how long he slept, and so on.

When he first arrived at the clinic he apparently slept only four or five hours a night. In the course of the evening he became increasingly uneasy and showed great reluctance to go to his room. He hung around in the corridor or, if the weather was mild, he would sit in the garden, where he was also sighted early in the mornings, long before anyone else had got up. As he requested night staff to lock him into his room every night, the only way he could have got into the garden at such early hours was by climbing out of the window. He would often sleep during the day.

Evidently he was frightened of the dark. He worked out all sorts of precautions, which would have seemed ridiculous had they not been so pathetic. For example, it was discovered that he leaned a wastepaper basket full of empty tin cans against the door, so that when it was opened the basket fell over and the noise of the cans cascading over the floor would wake him up. This was the "burglar alarm." He kept the window of his room locked throughout the night. Sometimes he was found sleeping under the bed.

He didn't behave like someone occupying a room. He camped there, his bag always packed, ready to go. Of course he was in the room, but he had so little to do with it that one somehow thought of him as not occupying the same space as the room.

Considering the filthy state he had been found in by the police, his keepers had expected that the boy would not be very hygienic in his habits, but the reverse turned out to be true. He washed or took a shower several times a day. The nurse noticed that the skin of his hands was chafed and sore; apparently this was due to his excessive use of a nailbrush and pumice stone. All his sense faculties were acute, and he was particularly sensitive to smells. It was impossible to find out when he went to the lavatory. Despite close surveillance, he always managed to keep this a secret.

Perhaps the most striking evidence of the state of mind of Thomas N. at this time was his reluctance to be outside in bright sunlight; he seemed to be acutely disturbed by the presence of his own shadow on the ground beside him.

Most of these symptoms became less marked as time went on, and some of them finally disappeared altogether.

*B*ut as soon as Thomas was back inside the safety of his own room he took out the note which the man had slipped into his pocket during supper. It read:

"I've got some important news for you. Come to the shrubbery behind the old washhouse after dark."

The note was unsigned.

Whatever the important news was, the man obviously wanted their meeting to be kept secret. He had only looked at him once, pressing his forefinger against his lips as he reached out and dropped the note into his pocket. They had not exchanged a word.

He screwed up the piece of paper and put it in the wastepaper basket. How dark was dark? He sat waiting, looking out of the window. When he could no longer make out the roof of the big house beyond the wall he got up and left the room. Twenty minutes had passed since he had come out of supper.

Just as he reached the end of the corridor it occurred to him that someone could quite easily pick the note out of the wastepaper basket and read it. He wondered whether to go back. How long would the man wait in the shrubbery? He decided it was more important to destroy the note first, even if the few minutes' delay might mean missing his appointment.

He hurried back to his room, retrieved the note and burned it in the washbasin, letting the tap run until not the slightest trace of it remained.

It was only when he made his way back outside that he realized with dismay he had no idea where the washhouse was. The clinic was a vast place, with various annexes and outbuildings sprawling through the grounds. The washhouse might be in any one of these buildings. There was nothing for it but to walk all the way around.

As he skirted the back of the building he saw a match being struck in the darkness some way ahead of him. Someone was lighting a cigarette. Feeling sure it must be the man, Thomas decided to follow him.

The lights were on in the annex beyond. Instead of turning off along the passage that ran between this annex and the main residential building, as Thomas had been expecting him to do, the man followed a path leading along the annex wall in the direction of the garden. This puzzled him. It didn't seem likely that the washhouse would be in such an out-of-the-way corner of the grounds.

Through the windows of the annex where the lights were on he caught sight of piles of boxes and packing cases. Men were still working there. Apparently it was a storeroom.

Once he had passed the storeroom it became pitch-dark, but he could just make out the outline of another building beyond. He heard the sound of a door being forced open. After a while a muffled light splashed softly over the ground some distance in front of him. The door of the building the light came from stood ajar. He went in.

The source of the light was a single bulb suspended about a yard above the floor. A man who had been stooping to wrap a piece of rag around the bulb straightened up and tiptoed over to him, rubbing his hands.

"Come on in! Come on in!"

The tone of voice was jaunty, even exuberant, so that Thomas at once began to feel more at ease.

"So you found your way all right."

"Only by chance. If you hadn't lit that cigarette—"

"But I *did* light a cigarette. You see? So it definitely wasn't by chance."

"But you're not in the place where you said you'd be. The note said: Meet me in the shrubbery behind the washhouse."

"No, the old washhouse. Come to the shrubbery behind the *old* washhouse. That's what it said. The washhouse they use now is somewhere quite different. No mistake. Just have a look at my note."

Thomas felt uncomfortable. I've got some important news for you. Come to the shrubbery behind the washhouse after dark. Those were the words he had read. Then he had thrown the note into the wastepaper basket.

"Have you got my note with you?"

And after that he'd burned it. So he would never know.

"Anyhow," the man went on breezily, "that's neither here nor there. The main thing is that you've come. You see, if you hadn't come, then I wouldn't have had any news for you. That's why I chose this inconvenient spot. You've no idea what I'm going to say to you, and yet you take the trouble to come. Because you're *expecting* news, eh? You're expecting *tidings.*"

"Tidings!" echoed Thomas.

His heart began to beat a little faster. He made an effort to suppress the feeling of regret for having burned the note, and to pay very close attention to what the man was saying, as if his life depended on it.

"I say tidings, because it's not just ordinary news I've got for you. Oh no! Something much bigger than that. More in the nature of an—epiphany!"

"What's an epiphany?"

The man looked at him in astonishment and quite unexpectedly burst into a guffaw of laughter. Somehow this laughter didn't seem to belong to the man at all, and Thomas briefly had the impression that it must have come from somewhere else in the room.

"One always betrays oneself sooner than one thinks. Looking at me you'd never think I was a vicar of Christ's church," went on the man, ignoring his question, "and you'd be right. I'm not. But you also wouldn't guess that I once had been, eh?"

"No," said Thomas.

"Well, I once was. Dog-collar dog's life, gave it up along with my wife: bad habits both of them. That's it in a nutshell."

The man clapped his hands and laughed, leaned back against the table and scratched his crotch.

"Does that shock you?"

"What's an epiphany?"

"Yes, I was coming to that. An epiphany is not something I can explain. It's something I must show. Something that is shown to you. And I can assure you that once you've seen it your whole life will be transformed—*if* you see it, that is. For you must realize that although it's shown to many, it's seen by only a few."

"Have you seen it?"

"Oh yes indeed. Many times."

He smiled happily, stretching his arms. Thomas noticed his dirty fingernails, dirty cuffs and stained sleeves.

"Why did you give up being a vicar? Was it because of seeing the—?"

"Quite. As a matter of fact, I was given the sack. It made no odds though, since I'd have left anyhow."

The man paused, and as he seemed to be thinking Thomas waited in silence. He had no doubt that something extremely important was about to be communicated to him.

And after a while the man started speaking again in his sprightly manner.

"Like most people, my life began with . . . ah . . . well, with my *parents,* of course. My father was a bishop. When I was a small child, my mother used to get him to bring home from the office any old surplices that were no longer needed, and she would make them up into nightgowns for me. So from the very start I wore the church next to my skin. Can you imagine it? Needless to say, they were most uncomfortable. You can never really wash the starch out of a surplice and the material is rather coarse, you see. No wonder I hated the things.

"Every evening she would take me into my father's study and stand me on the table. My father waited with his back to the fire, one hand resting on the mantelpiece. Now then, little man, he would say. And I would begin. I had to recite something from the bible or the book of common prayer. My father was especially fond of the litany. So before I was five I could sort out words like *schism* and *slander* without any trouble at all. Fortunately I had a good memory. My father didn't punish me when I got stuck, but nonetheless I was frightened of him.

"The fact is, I had a guilty conscience, which was all the fault of that surplice. I had an unusually well-developed *organ* for my age, you see, and with every move I made the thing seemed to get . . . hooked up. God knows, perhaps it would have been better if I'd been uncircumcised," he gave a sigh, "less sensitive and perhaps not caught so easily. But in my family that would of course have been unthinkable. Well, be that as it may, my first erections were associated with surplices, and whenever I stood on the table in my father's study I was scared *stiff* it might happen.

"I never seemed to get out of surplices. As soon as I was out of nightgowns I was packed off to school and started wearing the real thing in church—it was a choir school, you see. I spent six years there. And so the first thirteen years of my life were spent in churches, one way and another. There was never any question of my having to choose a career. Naturally I would join the family business. I didn't require a vocation. It didn't matter to me that I had no strong feelings about god. But don't misunderstand me! The church meant a great deal more to me than just an old habit I couldn't get out of. I was fascinated by it, though I'm sure you won't guess why—"

"No," said Thomas, feeling that a response was expected of him. He was anxious for the man to come to the point.

"No?" repeated the man gleefully. "Well, I shan't keep you in suspense. I was fascinated by the *sensuousness* of the church.

"Now that's something an outsider could never understand. The catholics, of course, have always been very strong on it, and no doubt that's why they're still able to field a much better team than we. That's what really packs them in. Especially the women. The charms of our bawd and the holy goat —irresistible! What an infamous trinity! For there's one more, isn't there, who easily gets left out because there's no image of him: the tupmaster general, the ecstasy-giver panting in a cloud, smooth-tusked, with blubbering haunches and streaming flanks. Horruph! My goodness!"

The man became so excited that for a while he was unable to go on.

"Having been ordained, I duly arrived in my country

parish, and after I'd been doing the job for a few years I saw what a big mistake I'd made. I was now married, by the way, and—well, *that* turned out to be a big mistake too.

"At about that time, a new family moved into the parish. There was a daughter, a girl of fifteen. Antonia was her name. As luck would have it, her parents wanted her to be confirmed, and I was naturally given the job of preparing her. She was my only candidate. Came over to my house once a week, for the best part of a year, and I prepared her in my study. That's the advantage of being a vicar. Everybody assumes you're on the level. What other strange man's house would you allow your teenage daughter to visit one evening a week out in the wilds of the country? Yes, you see, the job definitely has its perks.

"This thing with Antonia began very slowly. At first I'd just thought of her as an attractive girl. It wasn't until she'd been confirmed and started coming regularly to communion that the relationship took on a different aspect. *This is the body and the blood* . . . It's always seemed to me that the eucharist is in a class of its own. By far and away my favorite part of the liturgy. Maybe that's attributable to my first contact with religion, and I mean *contact* quite literally. I first became aware of it through the sense of touch. My mother was aloof, I'd hankered for bodies, for palpable flesh, ever since I was a child. Celia, my wife, was cerebral and the godhead—with only a token appearance in the sacrament—really very insubstantial. And that's the rub, so far as I'm concerned; the spirit is either manifest in the flesh or not at all.

"And that is why, when I suddenly saw Antonia kneeling at the rail one morning, it was like a vision. She was no great beauty, but she had a splendid body and magnificent lips, which parted slowly, her tongue gliding out stealthily, moist, almost snail-like. Her tongue was a pure shade of pink, her teeth very white. Like a shell, her mouth, white at the opening with a gradual flush of pink. Her tongue curled under the wafer and drew back into its shell. Her face closed in on itself and seemed to be shining. She hungered for the sacrament, with a real desire. Christ's handmaiden she, no doubt of it! At such moments there was this curious mixture in my feelings for her, as if my soul had dropped into my loins. Here at last was *flesh.* And in it the spirit had become manifest, extreme and scattering bright."

The man sighed again and fell silent for a long while.

"So it went on, for two years. The purpose of my life came to be concentrated in a ritual lasting a few seconds, for my part never consummated, during early communion every Sunday morning. The eucharist alone would never be enough. I needed more.

"I suggested to Antonia's father that his daughter join the choir. He thought it was a good idea, in principle; there was the practical objection that she couldn't sing three consecutive notes in tune. From my point of view that was the great merit of the plan. She needed *training,* I said. That's how we got started on singing lessons. But can you spare the time, vicar, he asked. I said I'd manage to squeeze it in somehow.

"The singing lessons went on all summer in a little room at the back of the schoolhouse. It turned out that Antonia could play the piano rather nicely. Very well, I said, shall we play some duets? And so we began to play duets. And every now and then her father would stop me in the road and ask, Do you think Antonia will be good enough to join the choir, vicar?— He always said 'vicar' to me, almost as if to reassure himself that I was everything I appeared to be. Surely, I said, it won't be long now. For by this time Antonia was standing with one hand resting on my shoulder when she sang her arpeggios, and quite soon after that she was sitting on my knee while she practiced her scales. It was one of the hottest summers in years. And now there was talk of Antonia going away to music school the following spring, and whenever I ran into her father down at

———

the bank or the post office he would ask anxiously: But do you think Antonia will fill the bill? Antonia will fill anything, I replied. For by this time those long burning afternoons were beginning to cool, and a little wind came through the open windows, making the music sheets rustle on top of the piano, and Antonia would suddenly turn and look up at the sound, her breasts *startled*, pitching and pealing, just like bells, so that I'd have to smother them with my hands and make them still.

"It was during these months that the vicar's mind began to take a queer turn. There was a sermon I gave which didn't go down too well, even provoking a letter from my bishop. The sermon was about the medieval theory of the virgin conception by the ear. Not the sort of subject for your rural flock, the bishop said. Nobody could know it was Antonia I was talking about. In the world around me I began to see the contours of her body. I wanted to get into her, every wrinkle, slot and cranny, her ears, her buttocks, the crook of her arm and the sockets of her eyes. I would feel I was plunging into her from a great height. Her belly caught me like a net. It was whippy and full of spring. I'd ask her if she wanted the sacrament, and she'd say yes, and I'd shove it right into her gut. It was the sacrament all right. It detonated deep inside her, her belly was awash with it and it shone out of all the pores of her skin."

The man suddenly broke off, stepped quickly forward and turned out the light. Thomas heard a door opening, and then the sound of voices. After a while it again became still. The man must have been standing very close to him, for Thomas could feel his heat, like a pulse, coming to him out of the darkness.

He switched on the light, glanced at his watch and turned the light out again.

"We have to be very careful, you see. We still have another five minutes, but we'd better go. It's always punctual."

"What's punctual?"

"You'll see."

The man opened the door and Thomas followed him out. They made their way cautiously back past the storeroom. The lights were out now. It occurred to Thomas that the men whose voices they had heard must have finished work and gone home for the night.

On the far side of the main building they came out onto a lawn where Thomas had not been before. The man squatted down with his back to the building and lit a cigarette under his jacket.

"What happened?" asked Thomas after a while. "What was the end of the story?"

"The end of the story?"

The man squatted on the lawn smoking his cigarette. Thomas watched the glowing end flare and fade.

"Well," said the man, "I was through with the church. For the reason, oddly enough, that I'd finally become a religious man. It all came to an end, as it was bound to, one evening in March, not long before Antonia was due to leave. We were in the church. I was practicing organ voluntaries and she was turning the pages for me, when I suddenly broke off and said to her, Antonia, let's do it on the altar. And d'you know, she didn't bat an eyelid. I had her up there before you could say the bawd's prayer. And when I saw her buttocks against the dark velvet of the altar cloth, fleshed out, smooth and perfectly white, I thought to myself, there's that shell again, and it came over me very strong. But just at that moment the door of the sacristy opened and the woman who used to do the church flowers came in carrying a bunch of daffodils."

The man rose to his feet and turned towards the house. He gave a gasp, as if he'd been hit in the stomach.

"There!"

Grabbing Thomas by the arm, he pointed to a window directly ahead where a light had just gone on. A woman passed the window, went to the back of the room and began taking off her clothes. Letting them lie just as they had fallen, she turned around and came right up to the window. She was a fat, plain-looking woman of at least fifty, with pendulous breasts and swollen legs. Folding her hands over her stomach, she took up position at the window and looked out, absolutely motionless. Thomas watched with amazement and disgust. The naked woman stood at the window as if she were made of stone.

"What's she doing? What does it mean?"

"She thinks she'll get a child."

"What?"

"She thinks she'll get a child," repeated the man impatiently, without taking his eyes off the window. He stood stock-still, leaning slightly forward, as if listening very intently.

"She has this idea that if she stands naked at the window at night she'll get a child. That's why she's in this place."

Thomas couldn't make head or tail of this and began to feel extremely uncomfortable.

"Why are you showing this?" he asked suspiciously.

"It's what I promised to show you," said the man. "It's an epiphany."

Thomas could hardly believe his ears.

"But it's just—"

He was bitterly disappointed.

The man began to chuckle and, as if this had been a sign, two white figures emerged from the passageway and stopped for a moment at the corner of the building. They were obviously looking for something. Thomas was in no doubt as to what that was, and that there was going to be an unpleasant scene, so he set off at once in the opposite direction as fast as possible. Behind him he heard peals of laughter ringing out through the night. Pausing at the far corner of the building he looked back and saw the two white figures striding rapidly and purposefully across the lawn.

A few days after Thomas N. ended his hunger strike he approached his nurse and began to question her about a rumor he had heard concerning an incident in the canteen.

She had no idea what he was talking about, but to set his mind at rest she said she would see what she could find out. To her surprise, he took her up on this offer very seriously. If she did so, he cautioned, then the matter must be kept secret; inquiries should be made in an offhand way, so that nobody would guess what she was really after. The nurse gave him her word. A little later, however, he came back and asked her to forget about the whole business.

The following day he again brought the matter up. He was now more specific. He said he had heard people complaining about certain patients who had caused some kind of disturbance in the canteen—it seemed they had been protesting about the food. He would now like to set the record straight. The rumor was nonsense. It was a complete exaggeration to say that what had taken place was any kind of disturbance. In fact, there had not been any protest about the food at all.

Thomas N. returned to the "incident," as he darkly called it, again and again, embellishing it here and there, but sticking to the basic story. By this time the nurse realized that her patient must be alluding to that lunch in the canteen when he had overturned a table and caused a lot of damage. The "incident" was obviously a confabulation based on this scene.

Dr. Ormond thought this was quite feasible. Confabulation was a typical symptom of patients with memory impairments; it was not so much lying as a confusion of things they had actually experienced with things they thought they might have experienced. Unlike such cases, however, the confabulations of Thomas N. seemed to be deliberate, even artful. The boy had a secretive nature, but at the same time he was motivated by a compelling urge to "show his hand." His nurse thought he was cunning. Possibly some of his confabulations were mere blinds, intended to confuse them.

The canteen incident was the first of many similar obsessions, some commonplace, some fantastic, which Thomas N. took up and discarded during the following weeks. Most of these obsessions were noted to have a tenuous connection with events that had actually taken place, and they would display certain patterns.

Most striking was a tendency to reconstruct these events in such a way as to cast doubt on whether they had in fact taken place at all. The remarkable fact was that the boy went to such elaborate lengths with these reconstructions, since the event itself was usually so trivial that nobody would even have been aware of it if he had not harped on about it himself. He drew attention to something that other people had not noticed in order to persuade them to forget about it.

One morning he complained that it was very cold, and refused to get out of bed. The nurse took his temperature and found that he was a bit feverish. He spent the day in bed.

By the following morning the fever had gone and he got up, although still looking rather pale. He seldom left his room, but whenever he did he wore his raincoat, complaining how cold it was. Meanwhile the spell of brilliant summer weather continued. For the next few days the sight of Thomas N. traipsing along the corridors in his shabby raincoat caused amusement. He wouldn't go outside on any account.

He became solicitous about the health of his nurse, offering her some rather curious advice. For example, she should avoid getting cold after swimming, and make sure that she didn't hang around in drafty places. That might be bad for her health. People easily forgot how chilly it could get on summer evenings. Did she sleep with the windows open? And did she draw the curtains carefully at night? It was impossible to be sure the curtains were properly drawn unless one also checked from outside.

It wasn't long before Dr. Ormond guessed the drift of the boy's questions. He had heard about the incident which had occurred a couple of nights previously, and from the patient who had been involved he learned that Thomas N. had been with him on the lawn in front of the window.

The gist of the story the man had told was true. As a result of repeated appearances in court on charges of indecent exposure and molesting women the disgraced cleric had been admitted to the hospital in the hope that something could be done for him. He had seen the light, quite literally, in a number of ground-floor windows, and he wanted others to see it too.

Dr. Ormond was particularly interested in the raincoat which Thomas N. had found it necessary to wear during hot summer weather. It was not a case, he thought, of the boy catching a cold and then putting on a raincoat, but of initially wanting to wear the raincoat and then catching a cold in order to make this seem plausible—he had even produced a temperature to justify it. In some obscure way the raincoat seemed intended by proxy for the naked woman in the window. But he would give them no help with the matter. When confronted with the story, he denied it altogether.

This last, very devious reconstruction brought a number of points into focus. In this incident, nakedness had been the apparent issue, but thinking over previous reconstructions of events, Dr. Ormond decided that the common denominator was of a more general nature.

All the reconstructions dealt with situations in which the boy had felt himself, in one way or another, to be *exposed*. They could be described as a kind of psychological revisionism, whose task was to modify unpleasant aspects of reality; specifically, to lessen the sense of exposure or even, if possible, to eliminate altogether the experience in which it had been felt.

At its most elementary level, Dr. Ormond concluded, the boy's fear of exposure was a fear of anything that objectively demonstrated his existence. When the strain of this task became too great, reconstructions were employed, like photographs which had been retouched, with one figure consistently defaced or excised.

In this undertaking the boy had been his own best ally. The solution had been absolute: he had lost his memory. All subjective evidence that he existed was obliterated. By his own peculiar logic, if nobody knew who Thomas N. was, it became rather doubtful *that* he was.

This analysis encompassed every aspect of his behavior; for example, the intake of food. He preferred it in liquified form, and his manner of eating it was surreptitious. He showed an interest in objects only when they were missing. A naked woman was covered up with a coat. Perhaps he was also repudiating aspects of sexuality in this episode; certainly, a pathological secrecy about his own body and all bodily functions had frequently been observed.

As with so many forms of neurotic guilt, the nature of the fear of Thomas N. was proleptic, not merely preceding but causing the situations from which it subsequently appeared to have arisen. Thus it came to reside in the unlikeliest, the most trivial of places. Paradoxically, the triviality of the object which it battened on was an essential aspect of this kind of fear. Even the patient himself would be bound to admit the disparity between the intensity of his fear and the harmlessness of its apparent cause. He created a certain amount of leeway for himself; there was more fear than necessary, and thus there would be no surprises, no being taken unawares.

This tendency to overcorrection, as Dr. Ormond saw it, was typical of persons suffering from a morbid sense of guilt. They took preemptive action, supplying feelings of guilt for which there was no immediate cause, in the hope of forestalling penalties they had learned to expect. In the case of Thomas N. Dr. Ormond had no idea as to the genesis of such feelings, but the form in which they were manifest was extraordinarily clear.

The boy felt guilty about his own existence. He behaved as if it were a secret he was frightened would be found out. He had suppressed his memory, and in so doing had contrived a shift of emphasis from what he had forgotten to the fact that he had forgotten, this in turn eliciting feelings of guilt and unease, which took the form of a remorseless inquiry into the antecedents of every here and now, day by day, minute by minute. It was a closed circuit, offering nothing but questions, endless questions.

Has something been forgotten? Something *absolutely vital* that was supposed to be remembered. The real state of affairs, what all this is really about. Have people been tipped off? In the canteen, for example. Did they see? Do they know? Do people *know?*

Thomas N. asked a lot of such questions, but Dr. Ormond was not able to give him any answers.

*T*he police inquiries into the case of Thomas N. were desultory. They had hundreds of persons on their files listed as missing in the metropolitan area alone.

A few days after the boy had been found an article

appeared in a local newspaper. It was accompanied by a photograph of him and the caption: Who knows mystery boy? The police withheld the information about a birthmark on the inside of his wrist, because public appeals of this nature always attracted their share of cranks. It was possible that people who had never even seen the boy might turn up and claim he was their child. The best way of disproving such assertions was to withhold the one piece of information any legitimate claimant would be bound to know.

On the morning the article appeared the police received a call from an elderly couple claiming to be the boy's parents. "Our boy beyond a shadow of doubt," said the father. He stated that the boy had run away from home a year ago. Since then they had not heard any news of him. Asked to describe any particular distinguishing marks, the man mentioned a scar on the arm. This description did not quite tally with the birthmark, but it was close enough to warrant further inquiries.

The callers turned out to be a mild, earnest couple in their late fifties. The wife, who did all the talking, showed the police officer around the house.

Her husband suffered from heart trouble, she said, and had been retired early several years ago. They had moved to their present address in the same year, living "a very quiet sort of life." It was a tiny house. Upstairs there were two bedrooms. The "son's" bedroom was in perfect order; his clothes hung neatly in the cupboard. The police officer noted, however, that these clothes were much too small, even if one made allowances for the fact that Thomas N. might have grown prodigiously in the course of the last year. In the sitting room downstairs the mantelpiece was lined with snapshots of a boy from infancy to the age of eleven or twelve. The subject of these pictures did in fact bear a slight resemblance to Thomas N., but the couple were unable to explain why there weren't any more recent photographs.

Further inquiries eventually established that the whole thing was a hoax. The ageing couple were in fact childless, although they would admit no more than that they had been "mistaken." Their fantasy about a son had apparently been kept up for a very long time, courtesy of a distant nephew whose photos could safely be put on view for the reason that he had been dead and buried for the past twenty years.

A few other calls from people who had seen or might have seen the boy were also followed up, but none of them led to anything. After the initial sensation of the appearance of the "mystery boy" interest in the case quickly declined and Thomas N. sank back into obscurity.

He was discharged from the clinic at the beginning of August after a stay of two months.

Qualified psychiatric opinion determined that the condition of amnesia was "chronic and, if not incurable, at least not susceptible to treatment." All attempts, including the use of drugs and hypnosis, had failed to uncover a single clue as to the boy's identity. The task had not been made easier by the patient's "intractable manner and refusal to cooperate." He was not regarded as constituting a hazard to public safety, so there was no reason to detain him longer. An understanding was reached with the police to the effect that there would be no prosecution on the charge of possession of drugs, provided that responsibility for the boy was taken over by an appropriate welfare organization.

Before Thomas N. left the clinic he had an interview with an officer from the local council.

Although the boy's exact age was not known it had been decided, in view of his "exceptional circumstances," that it would be best to assume he was still under seventeen, as he could then be received into care by the child welfare department of the council and placed in one of the department's own homes.

None of this seemed to interest the boy much one way or the other. He asked the welfare officer what sort of a place the institution was. Well, it was very nice of course, and for a start he would do better to call it by its proper name: it was not an institution, but a Home. It accommodated boys who had to be removed from their own homes by court injunction as a result of intolerable family conditions. Some of them attended school in the normal way, and some of them were in apprenticeship. As Thomas was assumed to be past the legal school-leaving age, the question of whether he attended school or went out to work must depend upon his aptitude. Unfortunately, in view of his "illness" it seemed doubtful he would be able to cope with the demands of a sixth-form curriculum, and for the same reason the jobs open to him might be rather limited.

How much did he know? Without knowledge he would not be able to get anywhere. In order not to raise his hopes unduly, the welfare officer suggested they take a realistic view and assume that he knew nothing. But he would arrange for tests to be made, and if it seemed likely that he would benefit from further education, and this could be satisfactorily funded, the final decision was up to him. The alternative was to apply for some vocational training or get a job. The welfare officer would help him in every way he could to find something suitable.

The move to the Home would only be temporary. As soon as the uncertainties about his future had been cleared up he would be free to look for accommodation elsewhere. The welfare officer knew of a number of approved hostels, for example, where he felt sure Thomas would soon settle down. Besides, there was always the possibility of his recovering and being reunited with his own family.

So there really wasn't anything to be worried about at all.

It was almost dark when Thomas was deposited at the gates of the Home. The porter directed him across the quadrangle to the main building where Mr. Girdon, the director, was expecting him in his office at the end of the corridor on the second floor.

Inside the main building it became even darker. It took him a while to find a light switch. He was standing in a long red-tiled corridor. There was not a soul to be seen.

He had never been in such a long corridor. There were doors leading off it all the way down. He pushed open the first door and went in. He found himself in an enormous room.

At the end of the room was a tall bay window with shattered glass. It had been broken on the inside; on the outside it was protected by a wire mesh. Along the walls there were built-in lockers, standing three tiers high, painted bright green. They must have been only recently painted, but the surface had already been plowed up by a terrific white scar running the entire length of the room. The doors of some of the lockers had been ripped out, hinges and all. A dozen rough tables, boards tacked on trestles, stood rammed up against the walls to clear a space in the middle. The area around this space was littered with cartons, scraps of paper and food. The room looked as if it had been blown apart by a bomb.

He made his way between the tables and opened one of the lockers. Almost as soon as he did so he regretted it, but having once started he found himself unable to stop. With a mounting sense of unease he went along all the lockers as fast as he could, opening every one of them. He did so mechanically, without curiosity, hardly even noticing what was inside. In one locker there was a bird in a cage. Hastily slamming the last locker door, he turned off the light and hurried out.

He had no sooner left the room than he began to doubt whether all the lockers were now shut. To set his mind at rest he went back in and had a second look. They all were.

"But were all the lockers shut in the first place?"

However hard he tried to remember, it was impossible to say for sure. And if one or two of them had been open, which ones? There was no answer to this. If anyone noticed that his locker was not as he had left it, then of course he must deny that he had ever been in the room. He might have stood there hesitating longer if it hadn't suddenly occurred to him that Mr. Girdon was waiting for him in his office at the end of the second floor.

"How stupid to have opened that locker in the first place!"

He had got off to a bad start.

Coming back into the red-tiled corridor, he noticed for the first time pictures of ships hanging on the walls. He walked the length of the corridor, looking at the pictures. They all showed old sailing ships. They seemed vaguely familiar.

But what puzzled him was that there didn't seem to be any way of getting up to the second floor. He thought the stairs would be at the end of the corridor, but it came to a dead end. He turned around and started to walk back. At that moment the lights went out.

He remained standing quite still. Perhaps because the lights were out he picked up the sound more easily, but he now had the impression that he could faintly hear a voice. It was a woman's voice. At first it seemed to be coming directly out of the wall. He groped his way along. After a few yards he caught sight of a strip of light at the bottom of a door just off the corridor. The door was a little way down a narrow passage, which he must somehow have overlooked, leading off the main corridor.

He went past the door, listening for the woman's voice, but he could hear nothing. At the end of the passage he tripped over a step. There must be a flight of stairs. So this was the way up to the second floor.

As he began to go up the stairs he heard the voice again, this time more clearly. He could understand individual words. If the voice had not been so clear he would perhaps have ignored it and gone on. He stood hesitating in the dark and thought about Mr. Girdon waiting for him upstairs. But there was no mistaking the fact that the woman he could hear talking in the room must be very close to the door, and for the time being this seemed to be the more important matter. He should definitely stop and listen. So he went and put his ear to the door. He could understand every word the woman said.

"Well, I got to this hospital, and in the first ward there were about four women, yelling their heads off. One of them, my goodness! she really did scream. Which was odd, since I was later told she was having her fifth child. She was a prostitute from the area down by the docks. Anyhow, I was taken into another ward, where it was dark, because I was the first to be put in there. And they gave me an enema and a sort of white apron, a nightshirt open at the back, like the ones they have at the barber's. The midwife said to me rather crossly, All right, you'd better get along to the lavatory, down there and left there and straight ahead there—and so off I went, barefoot, with this rag hanging down in front of my body. But instead of finding the lavatory I arrived in a big room full of men lying asleep, and it was dark, and of course by now I needed to get to the lavatory really badly, what with the enema and the child in me about to be born. There was an old man awake in this room, however, who was very kind, and he got up and showed me the way. After the enema had cleaned out my insides the midwife came back and had a look at me, in a way that would be strictly forbidden nowadays, for she simply reached into my vagina and said Yes, I can feel the penis of a baby boy. Off she went again, and I lay there singing a boy a boy a boy a boy a boy a boy softly to myself, and was very happy. I could see the midwife darting to and fro in the next room, and the other women there, some of them getting in and out of bed. And watching them made me somehow feel afraid, made me think it must be going to get a lot worse. I could see everything going on through a crack in the door. By then my condition was far advanced and so I called the midwife. Well, she asked in her gruff way, what is it? I was young and looked even younger than I was, so I felt a bit awkward, and all I could say was I don't know, but it all seems to be so different. The midwife didn't think that was much of an answer. She ripped the sheet from my body and banged on the light and saw at once that I was in fact already giving birth. She tossed the sheet back over me and snapped, Couldn't you have said so sooner? But I didn't have the slightest idea how it was all supposed to happen. And besides, the midwife had said it would take a good four or five hours. I'd been in there, what, only forty minutes or so. The midwife at once scurried off and came back with a woman doctor. She was very gentle with me. And in next to no time he was born. The doctor picked up the little bundle—it was so, yes, tiny. At first he didn't cry at all. And she laid him and the umbilical cord on my stomach, took a pair of scissors and said Bye, and cut the cord. This moment was somehow very festive. Then she put the little bundle on a table beside the bed, cleaned and swaddled him. I began to realize how cold I was. There can't have been any heating at all in the building. Apart from that,

---

I was exhausted after the birth. While giving birth I had lain uncovered for at least half an hour with only a scrap of white linen, a nightshirt on. I was shivering and my teeth began to chatter. The baby was tidied up, weighed and measured and laid in an enormous basket, all by himself, because he'd been born first, even though the other women had arrived long before me. This worried me a little. I was worried they might mix him up later on with one of the other babies. Although I'd had a good look at his face, hadn't I? I mean I wouldn't forget it, would I? Meanwhile a woman had started yelling in the next room. The midwife put out the light and was off in a trice. No wonder she was so thin, with all that rushing around. She was in such a hurry that she didn't even have time to close the door, so I was able to watch this woman lying opposite me in the next room who was right in the middle of giving birth. I could see a bubble, like a balloon, inflating between her legs. And the midwife came in with a needle and a bowl and pricked the bubble—a lot of liquid ran out into the bowl and out came the child too, just sort of slipped out. My boy was born at a quarter to—"

The voice broke off in midsentence. There was a sound rather like a click, followed by a long sigh. After a while Thomas thought he could hear someone moving about inside the room. He raised his hand to knock.

But at this moment a door on the floor above opened and shut. Thomas immediately started up the stairs.

As he started up the stairs he heard footsteps approaching from the far end of the corridor above. Noticing that one of his shoelaces was undone, he stopped at the turning of the stairs and bent down to tie it up. But his fingers were stiff and he fumbled. The lace was worn and kept slipping back out of the noose. All this time the footsteps were getting closer, and still he couldn't thread the lace through the noose. This gave him a feeling of such acute discomfort that he had difficulty not to urinate. He knotted the lace with a violent jerk, snapping it, and just as he straightened up somebody appeared at the top of the stairs. Thomas saw his boots first. He looked up and saw the rest of him. He was a very big man, completely bald, and he was frowning.

"Are you the boy Thomas?" demanded the man.

"Yes."

"What on earth have you been doing?"

"Trying to find the way here. And then this shoelace . . . this shoelace came undone."

He realized how feeble this excuse sounded, but it was already too late. The big man was looking at his watch and frowning even harder.

"What, twenty minutes? *Twenty minutes?*"

"Twenty minutes?"

"The porter rang twenty minutes ago and said he'd sent you over. Explain why you're so late."

"Well . . ."

Thomas thought about the bird in the cage and the pictures of ships hanging on the corridor walls. He realized it was going to be impossible to explain all these things.

"The light suddenly went out, you see. And the shoelace came undone."

The big man didn't look at all satisfied.

"You'd better come along with me."

Thomas picked up his bag.

"Really, the light suddenly went out, you see, and—"

But the big man had already turned back down the corridor. Thomas followed him up.

"I'm Mr. Girdon," said the man over his shoulder. "You know who I am. The director of the Home."

"Yes," said Thomas.

It sounded more like a warning than an introduction.

He followed Mr. Girdon down the corridor into a room

where a single light was burning over a massive desk. Perhaps the desk wasn't in fact all that large but only seemed so because the room was so bare. Mr. Girdon walked around the desk and sat down on the far side. And perhaps he isn't such a big man either, thought Thomas, but only seems so because of his bald head. He looked at Mr. Girdon and his desk and decided that the two somehow fitted.

Suddenly Mr. Girdon shot out his hands and cracked his knuckles.

"Do you know why you have come here?"

"No," said Thomas.

"Well have a think about it."

Thomas was at a loss. A quite irrelevant thought occurred to him: suppose Mr. Girdon were to put a hat on the desk. That would give him a very queer feeling.

He pulled himself together and concentrated on the question.

"Perhaps because there is nowhere else to go," he said at last.

"Good."

Mr. Girdon nodded encouragingly.

"All the boys at the Home are here for that reason. There isn't anywhere else for them to go. However, there's more to it than that. Isn't there."

"More?"

He was confused and found it difficult to concentrate on what the director was saying. To his unease, it seemed that Mr. Girdon was perfectly well aware of this too.

"That there isn't anywhere else for them to go may be the reason why boys come here. But that's not why they stay here. They stay here because the Home becomes somewhere. That's what the Home is about. It becomes a somewhere place for nowhere boys. Of course this takes time. Normally you would stay here for two or three years—"

"Two or three years! The welfare officer said it would only be temporary."

At this interruption the director blinked once very hard and looked at him severely.

"If you would let me finish."

After a deliberate pause, whose effect was not lost on Thomas, he went on.

"Normally you would stay here for two or three years. But you are not normal. Yours is a special case. The welfare officer has informed me of all the particulars. One thing I should like to be clearly understood: in the question of how long you are to stay at the Home, whether for only a short time or quite a long time, he has agreed to defer to my judgment. The final decision is up to him, but how he decides will be heavily influenced by my recommendation."

Mr. Girdon's way of saying this word left Thomas in no doubt that his recommendations were very seldom good.

"There are other contingencies to be taken into account. A boy may lose his memory, forget who he is, and so on. I don't know. But I do know that a boy doesn't simply emerge from thin air. He has his people somewhere, his family. And his family will want him back, won't they. They'll be distressed. What's happened to our boy, they'll be asking. They'll be moving heaven and earth to find him. They will have notified the police. Friends and relatives will have been called on to help. Don't you think so? Don't you think that's how one would expect them to react?"

"Of course," said Thomas.

"I think so too. And when on top of that a local newspaper with a circulation of at least twenty thousand publishes the boy's picture with the caption: Who knows this boy?—well, one can hardly doubt that it will only be a matter of hours, or at most days, before someone turns up to claim him. And that's just it. Nobody does. All these efforts produce nothing. Now doesn't that strike you as a bit strange? This forces us to consider another possibility. Maybe the boy's people are not moving heaven and earth. Maybe they're lying low."

Mr. Girdon paused, adding softly,

"Maybe his people don't in fact want him back at all."

He leaned back and cracked the knuckle of his index finger.

"There's the possibility that his people don't want him back at all. That may shock you, but I assure you it's not uncommon. It's true of many of the boys here at the Home. Their parents wouldn't want them back even if they were paid to. But your case is different. We know nothing about your past. This makes it difficult to decide what procedure to adopt. It's our job to equip the boys at the Home with new identities, you see. We teach them to forget who they were and where they have come from. Everything about their past is rotten. It stinks. We have to . . . fumigate our boys, in a manner of speaking. But what about this boy called Thomas N.? What about *his* past? Is it rotten? Do we fumigate *him?* Should we decide to scrap his past and make a completely fresh start? Or should we wait and see what turns up? Bearing in mind that what does turn up may be very unpleasant indeed . . . there are all these contingencies. You see, it's not easy."

"No," said Thomas, nodding his head. He hadn't realized there were all these complications.

"Our task becomes a great deal easier, however, when we can be sure that the boy we are dealing with is not trying to deceive us. How honest is this boy being with us, we ask."

Thomas gave a start.

"Completely honest," he said mechanically. But at once he thought of the lockers, and the woman's voice in the room at the bottom of the stairs.

"There are two kinds of dishonesty," continued Mr. Girdon, as if he had not heard him, "and in some cases saying something you know is untrue may be the less serious of the two. Not saying something, keeping something to yourself, is also a kind of dishonesty. Towards people who need information in order to help you, worse than dishonesty. Do you follow me?"

"Yes," said Thomas slowly.

"There's no hiding dishonesty. Not ever. You can *smell* it."

Mr. Girdon was looking steadily at Thomas' hands.

"Do you follow me?"

"Yes."

"Let's imagine someone comes to the Home for the first time. The walk from the gates to my study on the second floor normally takes three minutes. On his arrival at the Home this person is given clear instructions by the porter but, well, perhaps he is rather a stupid person. On top of that, he has bad luck. The lights go out. He has to switch them on again. His shoelaces come undone. He has to do them up again. All this takes a great deal of time. Let's say another seven minutes. Seven and three is ten. His walk takes him ten minutes. Plausible? Well, all right. After all, he's not in a hurry. But what are we to say when his walk takes him twenty minutes? You see what I mean? We can no longer be satisfied with excuses about lights going out and shoelaces coming undone. We're inclined to think, Now then, what's this fellow been up to? We suspect he might have been snooping around and poking his nose into all sorts of places. Perhaps we mind him snooping around, or perhaps we don't. But it's pretty clear *he* thinks we mind. And that's the interesting point. You see what I mean?"

"Yes," murmured Thomas, fascinated by the director's smooth white skull under the lamplight.

"So of course that sets us thinking and putting two and two together. We think of that walk from the gates to the room on the second floor, and we stretch it a bit, in fact we make it a great deal longer. We imagine it takes fifteen or sixteen years. You see? We imagine it takes fifteen or sixteen years. And we ask much the same sort of question. Well, what's he been doing all that time? And the funny thing is, we get much the same sort of answer too. Scrappy answers, little odds and ends of rubbish about suitcase keys and stale sandwiches. Shoelaces, in a manner of speaking. Always *beside the point.* Well now, that's a bit thin, we think. Surely there's more to it than that. Of course there's more. It's just that he's forgotten it."

Thomas began to realize that Mr. Girdon knew a great deal more about him than he did himself. And this had something to do with the effect on him of the director's very large, penetrating eyes.

"Always *beside the point,* you see. So somewhere or other there has to be a point for him to be beside. He remembers the shoelaces, he can pick out bits of scum floating on the surface, but not the stuff that's gone down to the bottom. *The base of the matter.* The sort of stuff he might have come across while snooping around. In the course of fifteen years or so we can take it he does quite a bit of snooping around. Actually he may just be getting on with the ordeal of living, but he thinks of it as snooping around and poking his nose in because he's got the idea into his head that the others *mind.* So he acquires the habit of playing his cards very close to his chest and not giving anything away. You see? Not giving anything away. That's still not enough, however. He takes it a step further. He 'forgets,' or rather, he declines to remember. For by his reckoning, what shouldn't happen doesn't happen, and so there's nothing to remember, because it didn't happen. —The possibility that his people don't want him back begins to sound quite plausible, don't you agree?"

"Why shouldn't his people want him back?" asked Thomas mechanically.

"Why not?"

Mr. Girdon cracked all his knuckles and laughed genially.

"My dear boy, for infinitely many possible reasons. Perhaps he was born illegitimately or at an inconvenient time, or the parents would have preferred a girl. Perhaps he was a sickly child, or a backward child, a noisy child, or a dirty child. Perhaps they didn't like the color of his eyes or the shape of his nose, or the way he buttered his bread and wiped his fingers on his sleeve. Imagine him standing at the kitchen door, a toady little creature with snot under his nose, whining and badgering for something, always whining and badgering. The list is endless. Many little reasons, accumulating over the years. With some people you can never tell. There's a boy at the Home whose father turned him out of the house one morning because he didn't like the way he walked across the living room. He'd just got sick of having the boy around. It's always the same story. But your case is not like these. As a matter of fact, it's altogether in a class of its own. For your punishment has been quite extraordinarily severe."

"Punishment?" murmured Thomas.

"They've taken away your past," went on the director easily. "What possible act of yours could have made them take away your past?"

He sat back in his chair, folded his arms and waited in silence.

Thomas stood as if he were transfixed. A very big fear emerged slowly inside him, like a mysterious dark flower, from the pit of his stomach, pushing up into his throat. The director waited, his arms folded, for a long time. It seemed as if he were looking at Thomas from a great distance, not so much at him as into him, as though he were peering into a bottomless shaft.

Suddenly he looked at his watch and got up abruptly.

"Have you had your supper?"

"No," said Thomas.

"Then I'll take you along to meet the Matron. I expect she'll be able to arrange something for you. Where you are to sleep and so forth."

Thomas followed the director back down the corridor.

*T*he Matron was a broad, dour woman with a face as stolid as a side of chilled ham.

"We've only room in the sick bay. It'll have to do," she said, unlocking the door and switching on the light.

There were three beds with iron bedsteads, each with a chair at the end. Thomas put his suitcase on the chair of the corner bed. It was a cot rather than a bed. The three cots lay there as bleak and chilly as three corpses, with their starched linen and meager grey woolen covers. He sat down.

"Don't touch," barked Matron.

She stood in the doorway, in a short-sleeved tunic, her bare arms folded.

"You're in the middle bed. It's easier to make up. Corner beds make extra work."

Thomas got up from the bed and opened his suitcase.

"What about the things?" he asked.

"Lay them out on the bed."

He arranged his few things on the bedcover with particular care, hoping that in this way they might perhaps look less shabby.

"It's not much," he said.

"*I* wouldn't buy it," said the Matron archly. "Shoes on the floor."

Thomas put the tennis shoes on the floor under the chair.

"Where's the pajama top?"

"There isn't one."

She looked at his belongings contemptuously.

"Well, what *about* your things?"

"Well," said Thomas uncertainly, "they ought to be put away somewhere, shouldn't they?"

The Matron gave a short dry laugh.

"Put away? This junk? Where? Do what you like with it, but I promise you one thing: I'm not having any of it in *my* cupboards. That's flat."

Thomas began putting the things back into the case.

"For heaven's sake, boy, not the pajama bottom."

"Where should it be put then?"

"In the bin under the table. And I daresay you'll need the shoes. Where are your wash things?"

"Wash things . . ."

He made a show of searching in his case. The Matron sighed impatiently.

"I suppose you haven't got any. Have they just picked you up off the streets? Well, I'll have to see what I can find. Come along with me."

He followed the Matron along the corridor to a room marked LINEN.

She took a bunch of keys out of her pocket and opened the door. There were cupboards all around the room. She moved from cupboard to cupboard, taking out various articles, unlocking and locking each cupboard as she did so. Then she went over to a table.

"Towel. Pajamas. Slippers, socks, flannel."

She slapped them down on the table one by one, like a fishmonger stacking a slab. She picked up the whole bundle and thrust it at him.

"Carry," she said.

They went out, Matron again locking the door behind her.

"Why do you always lock the door?"

"They steal. The washroom's this way."

She set off in the opposite direction at such a pace that

Thomas had to run to catch up with her. Reaching the end of the corridor, she chopped open a door and wedged her foot against it.

"Washroom."

He peered in. It was a bare room with a row of basins along the wall and a stone trough in the middle.

"Take care. When they're wet they get slippery. Accident last week. Five stitches."

She pointed to the wooden slats on the floor.

"Baths twice a week, Tuesday and Friday. The water's hot between six and nine."

"Where's the bath?"

The Matron jerked her head in the direction of the stone trough. Then she let the door swing shut and set off again at top speed. Farther down the corridor they passed a row of lockers marked Socks, Underwear, Shirts. As she passed, Matron jabbed a finger at each of the lockers.

"Dirties go in here. Every Friday. Don't roll the socks. Put them in loose, one at a time, and tuck the ends in. Make sure they're turned the right way out."

He followed her into the dispensary. A small, bony boy sat on a chair in the corner, picking his nose.

"What is it?"

"Cough," said the boy.

The word was hardly out of his mouth when he was seized by a violent fit. Matron went over to the shelf and took down a large mud-colored bottle. She uncorked the bottle and stood waiting, spoon poised, until the boy had disentangled himself from his cough.

"Can't I have something to suck?" he whined.

"Open your mouth," said Matron.

He opened his mouth and she plunged the spoon into his gullet. It went down like a sword. The boy's eyes narrowed

---

anxiously as they followed the course of the spoon down under the tip of his nose.

Matron took a notebook out of the table drawer.

"Have you been today?"

"No," he said sulkily.

"That's three times in a row. You know what that means."

The boy slunk out. Matron turned to Thomas.

"What about you? Have you been today?"

"Been where?"

"Opened your bowels."

Thomas said nothing.

"Can't wait all day," said Matron irritably. "Anyway, you *ought* to be old enough to take care of yourself."

She slammed the drawer shut, hitched up her tunic and strode back down the corridor in the direction of the sick bay, talking as she went.

"They've all just had supper. But the kitchens are still open, so I daresay there'll be something left over. I'll have a tray sent up."

Five minutes later a man appeared in the sick bay, carrying the tray that Matron had promised.

"Welcome to the Home," he said in a sad, refined voice as he set the tray down on a table in the corner. "Sausage and beans, and I'm afraid they are cold," he added with distaste.

"Welcome?"

Thomas looked up with a start. He was a small, almost dwarfish man with a dingy complexion and a most peculiar face. It looked as if it had been split down the middle and the two halves badly pasted together again. The cultured voice didn't seem to belong to this dingy face at all. The man returned his stare with a little nod, perhaps intended as a sign of encouragement, but because the two halves of his face were in such disagreement it was impossible to guess what he might have been thinking.

The man vanished without another word.

Thomas didn't touch his supper. He felt ill and tired. But there was no question of going to sleep. Too much had happened. There were so many important things he still had to think about, so many details to be borne in mind. Without undressing, he lay down on top of the middle bed and began to go through a mental list of the important things in the order in which they had happened.

The business of the lockers. How safe was that? Could he tick it off? Not yet. Suppose he were challenged: why was someone poking his nose into those lockers? Well quite: why? He had no idea why someone would want to do that. But what about the bird? What if it ran out of water? What if it died? Who would be to blame?

Reluctantly, with the sense of an urgent question left unanswered, he passed on to the even more serious problem of Mr. Girdon. Did Mr. Girdon know more than he was giving away? Tomorrow he would have to check whether the room with the lockers was visible from the corridor on the second floor. And what about the voice of the woman in that other room? Did he know about that?

And in any case: was it forbidden?

But of course all this was nothing compared with some of the other things Mr. Girdon had said. Was it true, what he had said about the boys at the Home? Maybe a boy's father didn't like the way he walked across the room one morning. And so he had taken away his past. It was as simple as that. What possible act? What *possible* act? Many little reasons, accumulating over the years.

"And how honest is this boy being with us?"

He realized there was nothing to be done about Mr. Girdon either. He would just have to be on his guard.

———

He thought about the Matron instead. Don't roll the socks. Put them in loose, one at a time. But it could easily happen that you rolled the socks without thinking. Constant vigilance, that was the only answer. He would just have to make very sure he *didn't* roll the socks. And tuck the ends in. But which ends? There was nothing you could tick off. Never. And the list would always get longer, day by day.

He was drifting off into an uneasy sleep when he heard the clock strike one.

"I was worried they might mix him up with one of the other babies."

He sat up with a start. Of course! Until that business had been cleared up none of the other questions could be settled either. The room off the little passageway would have to be investigated at the first possible opportunity.

———

When Thomas got down to the dining hall the next morning breakfast was already under way. A tall, thin man with a reddish mustache came up to him and announced that he was the assistant master.

"Are you the new?" he asked in a reedy sort of voice.

"Yes."

"You're late."

He stroked his mustache and consulted a list.

"Are you sick?"

"No."

The thin man frowned.

"Then why've you been put in the sick bay?"

"The Matron said there was no room except in the sick bay."

The man seemed quite pleased with this offering.

"Ah yes," he said, referring to the list again, "so the middle table on the left."

Thomas went over to the middle table on the left and sat down at the end of the bench.

There was a tremendous din going on in the dining hall. Nobody paid the slightest attention to him. He made himself as narrow as possible and kept his eyes on the plate in front of him. He had hardly begun to eat his breakfast when there was a heavy knocking sound. He looked around and to his astonishment saw the thin man thumping the floor with a long pole. All the boys immediately stood up.

"Dismiss!"

There was a general rush for the door. Five or six boys at the other end of the room remained behind to clear the tables.

"Boy!"

Thomas looked up with a start.

The thin man with the reddish mustache had called out to a small boy who was heading for the kitchen exit. The boy stopped in his tracks. The thin man disengaged a very long finger from his knuckles, rather as if he were unraveling it, and beckoned the boy, who very reluctantly made his way back across the room.

"Sir?"

The man docketed the lobe of the boy's ear between thumb and forefinger, making it very plain to the boy that he knew all about him and was now officially taking note of his contents; a position which left the boy with no choice but to address his answers into his interrogator's shirt cuff. The assistant master clearly knew how to deal with unsatisfactory boys. He held his other arm slightly away from the body, thus conveying the unmistakable impression of a man about to drop some offensive object into the rubbish bin.

"I was in the lavatory," Thomas heard the boy say.

"What-te? For one hour?"

The thin man's neck rose forward a few inches out of its collar. The owner of the neck cupped his ear with the other hand and stooped just a little, feigning astonishment.

"I had . . ."

"What did you have?"

". . . diarrhea," said the boy, eventually locating the word. Now that he'd got it he kept a tight hold on it. "Diarrhea. I had diarrhea. It was very bad. Honest."

"You had diarrhea," confirmed the thin man, twitching his nose. He had a way of pickling his vowels which made his sarcasm particularly sharp. "So you will come to the library half an hour earlier this evening. You will bring your black book, your compass, and your ru-ler. You will *not* go to the lavatory. You will come to the li-bra-ry," giving the boy's ear a little twist for good measure at each of these syllables. Was that quite clear? Yes, it was very clear. *Quite* clear? Very. And so the offensive object was finally disposed of.

After breakfast that morning the assistant master took it upon him to instruct Thomas in his first catechism. He learned some interesting things. It appeared that Thomas was now his surname. By pickling his vowels and drawing out the second syllable of the name the assistant master succeeded in conveying to him that the entire boy amounted to no more than a vulgar and offensive part of his anatomy. With a show of extreme distaste he continued to put this offensive part of the anatomy rather frequently into his mouth in order to explain the functions it would be expected to discharge, and admonished him to renounce all those filthy habits which had caused him to be impounded in the Home in the first place, *viz.* slovenliness, deceit, the unnatural and disgusting abuse of his own or any other's sexual organs, and a great many extraordinary matters which Thomas now heard of for the first time. Further, he was to be *examined,* that very morning, in the li-bra-ry at nine o'clock sharp-pe. What was the state of his ignorance? Thomas didn't know. Assuming the offensive part of the anatomy was in a position to satisfy the examiners, it would be expected to be at the gates of the Home every day at ten minutes past eight sharp-pe, not including Sundays, and would accompany others of its kind to the local school. Otherwise they would see.

Was that all clear? More or less. Did that mean more or less? He meant it was clear. Were there any questions? No. What-te, none? The thin man juggled his eyebrows. And so Thomas was disposed of too.

The form of the assistant master, erect, swaying almost imperceptibly like some frail, deadly poisonous fauna on the seabed, became visible to Thomas the moment he turned off the corridor into the library a few minutes before nine. He stood so close to the door that Thomas had to squeeze up against the shelves in order to get past.

The assistant master held a small notebook and a slim gold pencil.

"Sit down at the table there."

Thomas sat down. A sheaf of lined paper, a pencil and some printed matter, shiny and with an ominous smell, lay on the table in front of him.

"Look at page one. Read the rubric at the top of the page carefully."

Untethering his watch and chain he looked up at the clock on the wall, set his watch, and began to wind it up.

"I have now synchronized the clocks," he announced. "Are there any questions?"

"No," said Thomas. He hadn't read the rubric and he didn't know what a rubric was. He had been listening to the assistant master winding up his watch.

"It's four minutes past nine. You have three hours in which to answer the question paper. Do not leave any blanks. Attempt all questions. I shall come back and collect your answer sheets at four minutes past twelve."

And the assistant master left the room.

Thomas read the first page of the question paper and turned to the next. The variety of the questions astonished him. As he read on, his heart sank, and long before he reached the last page he saw clearly that there wasn't a single question he would be able to answer. The task was hopeless.

Attempt all questions.

He sniffed the paper. It must have been freshly printed.

Something about the smell of the fresh print started off other ideas, and quite soon he had forgotten all about the sheaf of paper and the pencil in front of him and the questions he was supposed to be answering. He got up and went to the window. Quite involuntarily he raised the sash, climbed out onto the ledge and dropped down onto the gravel path below. He found himself outside and walking along the path without the slightest notion of what he was doing. In fact it was not until he turned off the path back into the building, and realized he was again in the red-tiled corridor with the pictures of ships hanging on the walls, that he was reminded, it seemed without his own knowledge, of the vitally important matter he had decided the previous evening: the room off the little passageway must first be investigated, before any of the other urgent problems, and in particular those impossible questions he was now supposed to be attempting, could be given his attention with any hope of success.

He knocked softly and went in.

Somebody who was sitting at the window turned around as Thomas came in and looked up. It was the man with the peculiar face who had brought him his supper the previous night.

The man didn't seem to be surprised to see him, and not particularly interested either. He vaguely indicated a chair, and without a word turned back to the window.

It was a small, dirty room. The paint was peeling from the walls and there was a lot of dust on the floor. Apart from three chairs, which were lined up in a row facing the window, the room was empty. Apparently it had not been inhabited for a long time. Thomas felt puzzled and disappointed. An empty room was the last thing he had expected.

The man was sitting on the left of the three chairs, completely engrossed in the view from the window. Thomas sat down on the right and looked out. It appeared to be a very ordinary view. He wondered why it so interested the man.

Perhaps he would also be able to explain to him the mysterious voice he had heard last night.

After they had sat there for some minutes in silence, which for his part the man evidently had no intention of breaking, Thomas tapped him on the shoulder.

"Sorry to interrupt, but it's rather important . . ."

The man didn't turn around, but he nodded to indicate he was listening.

"Were you in this room last night?"

"I'm never here after five."

"Is it your room?"

"No."

"Does anybody else come in here?"

"Not to my knowledge."

"You see, there was a woman talking in here last night."

The man turned round and scrutinized him.

"Was there? Are you sure about that?"

"Quite sure."

The man thought about this for a while.

"Well, there's no reason why you should lie. But how reliable is your memory?"

He turned back to the window.

"And what was this woman talking about?"

"About having a child. About giving birth."

"Who was she talking to?"

"Well, it didn't seem she was talking to anybody in particular. . . ."

The man glanced at him doubtfully.

"She was in here talking to herself? About giving birth?"

He pursed his lips.

"It might have been a woman in here. On the other hand, it might equally well have been a man."

"A man? But it was a woman's voice."

"A man listening to a tape recording of a woman's voice, you see."

This possibility hadn't crossed Thomas' mind. He suddenly remembered the click he had heard when the voice fell silent.

"Anyway, why does it matter?"

"It matters," said Thomas slowly, "because that was the first of a number of odd things that have been happening here which ought to be cleared up. You see, if there were an explanation for why that woman was talking in here last night, then one would be a lot surer of one's ground, generally, you see. Who was she? And who would she be talking to about giving birth? And whose birth? If there were answers to these questions one could be much more certain where one stood. As it is . . ."

"Why didn't you go in and ask, instead of waiting until this morning?"

"There wasn't time."

"That was very unfortunate."

Thomas took this to mean that the man didn't believe him.

"Theoretically, of course, there's no reason why someone shouldn't have been in here last night, but, well, just take a look at this room. It speaks for itself, you might say. And quite apart from whether there *was* someone in here or not, we still have only a tiny part of the evidence we would need to be able to answer the kind of questions you are interested in. You didn't see the woman. You only heard her. Perhaps if I'd been there I would've heard something different and would want to ask different questions. And as you say, you've no idea who this woman was, who she was talking to, or anything but what she happened to be saying at the time, which is just a fragment from an enormous complex. We need the context of what she was saying. You're asking rather a lot, you see."

The man thought for a moment.

"Still, perhaps the situation's not entirely hopeless. You say that if there were answers to these questions one would be more certain where one stood. But I should like to put it to you differently: if you were more certain of where you stood, then there might perhaps be answers to your questions. Even then, such answers would still only be provisional, in a manner of speaking, only adequate for yourself, since the answers you get depend very much on where you stand."

This was a quite novel aspect to the situation. Although the man did not sound very encouraging, at least he seemed interested in Thomas and to take his problem seriously.

"But how does one set about knowing where one stands?"

"Well," said the man cautiously, "the only way I can answer that is to tell you how *I* set about it, and I'm afraid I haven't made much progress so far. In fact, I'm not able to tell you—with any confidence—about anything much more than the rather," making an apologetic gesture, "limited view I have from this window, although even that could only be acquired with great patience and considerable labor; and I am so far from knowing what it is I have a view of that I can still only afford to consider where it is I have that view from."

He indicated the three chairs.

"The seating arrangements give you some idea of the difficulties I am encountering. Just sit there awhile and have a look."

The window looked out onto the street, with what appeared to be an office building opposite. Thomas sat and watched for a few minutes, but so far as he could see it was really a very ordinary sort of view.

"You see, I am by way of being a professional street-watcher," said the man. "In fact I think I can claim, without exaggeration, to be the world authority on the view from this window. Of course, it makes no odds whether it's from this window or from any other. It's the principle that counts. I say principle, because there are always three points to be borne in mind. What's being looked at, who's looking, and where he's looking from. Change any one of these and the view becomes quite different."

To make his point clear he invited Thomas to move to the other chair.

"You will find that you now have a slightly altered view. There is of course no such thing as the complete view. However . . . in an attempt to approach at least that ideal of completeness one can compromise by changing one's viewpoint from time to time. The most important thing about a view is not actually something in the view at all. What really matters is the frame. Once you have a frame you've also got a view, or to put it differently, without frames there are no views. The sense in which the frame can be regarded as the indispensable condition of the view is illustrated by the case of an acquaintance of mine, whose frame was a cage."

Thomas couldn't make head or tail of this.

"A cage? What do you mean?"

"This acquaintance of mine," said the man, ignoring Thomas' question, "was a political. People didn't agree with his ideas. In fact, when his ideas went beyond a certain point they didn't have to think twice about locking him up. It doesn't matter what he'd done. They locked him up for quite a long time. When he eventually got out he decided to go abroad. He went to a country where there were a lot of people who agreed with his ideas. He got a bit of a hero's welcome, I can tell you. He was invited to stay at a very nice villa by the sea. This villa belonged to a wealthy man who had a lot of influence. He also had sympathy with the ideas of this acquaintance of mine. So he ought to have been perfectly satisfied.

"But he wasn't. It was all right to begin with. He sat by

the swimming pool sipping iced drinks. And every morning his host would come along and give him a big smile and clap him on the shoulder.

" 'You're free!' he'd say.

"Things went on like this for a couple of months. My friend began to get restless. He was a bit fed up with having iced drinks down at the pool. He started getting up late in the mornings. His host didn't mind. He was a perfect host. He came along to my friend's room instead. He always said the same thing.

" 'You're free!'

" 'But what shall I do?' asked my friend one morning, as he stared at the ceiling. He stared at the ceiling to avoid looking at his host, whose breezy manner had begun to get on his nerves.

" 'Be free! Do what you like!'

" 'Unconditionally? Is that possible?'

" 'Of course!' said his host. And he went away roaring with laughter.

"So my friend got up and did what he liked. But he was a suspicious man. He was sure there had to be a catch to it somewhere. He turned his room inside out to see if it was bugged. He didn't find anything. He left a hair across the door of the cupboard where he had all his papers. Nobody disturbed it.

"Most people would have left it at that. Not my friend. He carried his search out into the garden. He combed every yard of that garden, and it was a biggish place. He thought he'd find tripwires and alarms and all sorts of secret installations. But he didn't. There were just the flowers, the insects and the grass. It was a free country.

"One morning, while he was taking a stroll in the garden, keeping his eyes skinned as usual, his host came out and joined him.

" 'Well,' he said cheerfully, 'are you satisfied?'

"He didn't have any objection to my friend searching the garden. He wanted him to do as he liked.

" 'Oh yes,' said my friend. But he sounded rather doubtful. 'And the air here is marvelous.'

"He stretched out his hand and tried to grasp the air.

" 'What's the texture of this?'

"His host shrugged.

" 'Why, whatever it's believed to be.'

" 'Incredible,' said my friend. 'Too good to be true. What if there's disagreement? Who's the arbiter?'

" 'There's never any need for one.'

" 'What of the state?'

" 'Perished!' said his host, lighting a cigar.

"My friend thought about this for a while.

" 'What of law?'

" 'By whom? For whom?'

"My friend thought again. His host puffed away cheerfully at his cigar and placed a flower in his buttonhole.

" 'What of God?' asked my friend at last.

"His host smacked his thigh and laughed so much he almost choked. He was such a good-humored fellow, and laughed so infectiously, that my friend couldn't help laughing either.

" 'That was a good one,' said his host finally, wiping his eyes with a large silk handkerchief.

"But my friend sobered up pretty quickly.

" 'No offense, of course, but you know: this isn't a very easy spot to be free in. That's what I've been wanting to say to you.'

"His host put on his broad-rimmed straw hat and smiled expansively.

" 'But of course, my dear friend. I understand perfectly. Perhaps you should try somewhere else.'

"And patting his guest affectionately on the arm he went off to tour his estate.

"Soon after this conversation the rich man had to leave his estate and spend a few weeks on business matters in town. He left a note on the table. It was quite brief.

" 'Dear Friend, please relax. You're free. Do whatever you like.'

"He was such a kind and generous man. But my friend became very angry when he read this. He tore the note into little pieces and flushed them down the lavatory.

"He started to take long walks. It was beautiful country, open heathland along the coast, with wild shrubs in bloom all the year round. But the farther he went the less he liked it. His walks became shorter. He would skirt around the house, for hours on end. Finally he just pottered about in the garden. He measured it out. It was too big. So he restricted himself to the lawn at the back of the house. He still wasn't quite satisfied, however. Just below the lawn, out of sight of the house, was a little hollow ringed with trees, and a patch of turf in the middle, perfectly level and smooth. When he saw this place he was delighted.

" 'This is just the spot for me,' he said.

"It was about fifteen feet square.

"It was here that Mr. Alkazenidor (for this was his host's name) found him when he arrived back home. He was so busy walking up and down and counting and measuring and hammering little stakes into the ground that at first he didn't notice his host. Alkazenidor stood quietly under the trees, nodding and smiling indulgently.

" 'Well?' he called out at last.

"His friend looked up, a little sheepishly.

" 'Ah. There you are. I'm just staking a claim. You don't mind, do you?'

"Alkazenidor spread out his hands, looking rather pained.

" 'My friend, why do you ask? All this is yours.'

"And he gestured to the sea and the sky.

" 'Thank you,' said his friend, 'but I don't want all that. What I want is a place. Look, I've been measuring it out. Do you think it's a place? D'you think it's got the feel of a place?'

"Hearing the slightly anxious note in his friend's voice, Alkazenidor immediately came out into the clearing and paced it out. He noticed that it was smaller than the amount of space which could have been at his disposal. It measured ten feet square.

"Of course he reassured him that it was a place.

" 'The limits give me scope,' explained his friend.

" 'It's a good place,' said Alkazenidor.

"His friend was very pleased, and the two men made their way back to the house in the best of spirits.

"There was a big truck standing in the drive.

" 'What's in that truck?'

" 'Equipment,' replied Alkazenidor. 'Come and have a cocktail.'

"The next morning he went with his friend down to the patch of turf among the trees. A large object was standing there under a black tarpaulin. Alkazenidor uncovered it. The object was made of steel, and it glittered in the sun. His friend looked at it in astonishment and walked around it a couple of times, as if he couldn't believe his eyes. But there was no mistaking what it was.

" 'It's a cage,' he said at last.

" 'It has the advantage of being seen to be so,' said Alkazenidor.

"His friend couldn't resist entering the cage. He paced it out. It was ten foot long and five foot wide.

" 'It's a nice fit,' he said grudgingly.

"Alkazenidor went away. His friend stayed all day in the little hollow examining the cage, and at sundown Alkazenidor returned.

" 'Well?' he asked.

" 'I suppose it's a way.'

" 'The only one,' said Alkazenidor genially. And with a smile he began to explain.

" 'The cage is a device of classic simplicity. It is able to arouse in the prisoner intimations of freedom of incomparable clarity and power: were he but free, he would be free. This ideal has suffered a decline in recent years. Standards must be kept up. In order to keep them from slipping irrecoverably we have had to have recourse to the cage. Certain of our clients, who are uncompromising purists in such matters, have expressed satisfaction with the cage as being of great assistance to them in the prompt and complete recovery of their appreciation of freedom. We would be happy to put it at your disposal. Now that you have had an opportunity to examine it at your leisure, what is your opinion? Do the arrangements give satisfaction?'

" 'It certainly seems solid enough,' said his friend, giving the bars a shake.

" 'Are there any aspects of security you feel to be deficient?'

" 'No, no . . . admirable, really.'

"Alkazenidor took a key out of his waistcoat pocket.

" 'Before I lock the cage, however, it is my duty to warn you—'

"His friend waved him aside.

" 'For obviously there is a condition,' said Alkazenidor with a laugh. 'You will appreciate that once a client has committed himself and freely entered the cage, under no circumstances whatever can we allow him out again. It cannot be impressed too strongly on the client that, although he will be cared for in all the necessaries of life, however terrible his remorse, however desperate his pleas, having once entered the cage he will remain there for the rest of his living days. Is that absolutely clear?'

" 'Of course, of course,' said his friend impatiently.

"Alkazenidor locked the cage and walked back to the house.

"It all happened just as he had said. In the evening, as he sat on the terrace sipping a cocktail, Alkazenidor could hear his friend beginning to curse and rave.

"When the breeze blew up from the sea, words and snatches of phrases were intelligible to him. They were the same words and phrases night after night, the same accusations, demands, pleas. But at about this hour it tended to get chilly, and Alkazenidor went back inside to have his dinner."

Thomas was puzzled and disturbed by this curious story.

"So he never got out?"

"If he had got out he would no longer have been free. He needed the cage for his particular point of view."

"But that's impossible!" protested Thomas.

In the distance a clock began to strike.

"Every view is from inside some kind of cage," said the man.

Thomas listened to the clock striking and jumped excitedly to his feet.

"Surely it can't be that late already? Was that eleven or twelve?"

The man hadn't counted the strokes of the clock either, and as Thomas could not risk taking any chances he took his leave hurriedly and at once made his way back. But he was so preoccupied with what he had heard, and what it was supposed to mean, and whether it answered any of his questions, that he took the wrong turning somewhere and lost his way, so that he climbed back through the library window with only seconds to spare.

At about this .time Thomas stopped having his meals with the other boys in the dining hall. An announcement to this effect was posted on the Director's Notice Board. Thomas hadn't known that such a board even existed, and if one of the other boys had not drawn his attention to the notice he would have missed it.

The notice was headed Scullery, and consisted of only one line: Until further notice Thomas will take his meals in the scullery. "Thomas" was underlined.

No reason for this decision was given. On making inquiries he was told it was merely an administrative problem; because of overcrowding in the dining hall somebody had to be moved out to the scullery, which happened to be the most convenient place available. Thomas had no objection to the scullery as such, and he didn't mind having his meals on his own either, but the explanation he was offered didn't satisfy him.

After the assistant master had come to the library that morning to collect the examination papers, which he placed and sealed in a large brown envelope, Thomas did not give the matter a second thought. He had simply not been able to answer any of the questions, and that was that. But as a result of the Scullery decision and a number of other changes in his life at the Home he began to suspect that everything was not quite as it should be, and to seek a reason for this. Perhaps the authorities were taking a much more serious view of the examination than he had; and if he had tried a little harder, he might have been able to answer at least one or two of the questions. He had to admit that. And it seemed that something in the nature of an admission was expected of him, for it gradually became clear from the changes now taking place that he was in fact being punished.

It began with his being told to report to the lodge, where the porter would give him odd jobs to keep him busy. He duly went along to the lodge and asked what he should do. But the porter knew nothing about the matter. He was a morose, suspicious old man, and he thought the boy was just out to play a trick on him. He brusquely told him to clear off.

So Thomas went away, made certain that he had understood his instructions properly, and came back to the lodge again. He found the porter waiting for him with a small broom in his hand.

"Sweep the yard, then."

"Yard? What yard?"

The porter pointed to the school quadrangle: it was a huge area, almost an acre. This might not have mattered if the broom the porter gave him had not been so pitifully inadequate for the job. It was so small he had to bend double. It took him nearly all day to finish sweeping the yard.

That evening he dawdled over his supper, hoping to see the man who came to clear the tables afterwards, but to his disappointment he failed to show up. Perhaps it was his evening off. The following morning, when Thomas looked into the room off the little passageway, he suspected there might be a more sinister explanation. For the room was now quite empty, the three chairs by the window had gone.

He became quite certain that something was up when he opened his suitcase to check that nothing was missing, as he always did before getting into bed at night. All his things had gone. Instead he found a complete set of clothes he had never seen before. The only thing that remained was the wallet with the photograph of the woman inside. He immediately went along to the Matron to find out what had happened.

"Stolen indeed! You couldn't have given the stuff away. Be thankful for small mercies. We can't have you leaving us looking like a ragamuffin. Nobody would want to have you in the state you were in, and that's for sure."

"Leaving? What do you mean?"

"Well, you'll have to leave sometime, won't you. You're here to leave. But don't ask me," said the Matron cryptically.

And that was all he could get out of her. But the fact was, his own things had been thrown away and another set of clothes substituted. They weren't even new clothes. Whose clothes were they?

"For goodness sake, boy, *I* don't know. Count your blessings and shut up."

But they weren't *his* clothes. The idea of having to wear somebody else's clothes made Thomas extremely uneasy.

The following evening there was still no sign of the man who was supposed to clear the tables. After supper Thomas went along to the library to evening study hour, as he had done on the previous day. The assistant master had given him an algebra book and told him to read Chapter One, but not to attempt the problems at the end of the chapter.

"Leave them until tomorrow," he had said.

But when the assistant master read the roll call that evening, and the other boys began to settle down to work, Thomas' name had been left out. He went up and drew attention to the omission.

The assistant master looked at him with mock surprise.

"Are you telling me that I've made a mistake?"

And his voice moved up half an octave.

Thomas said guardedly he was sure the assistant master had not made a mistake. However, the fact of the matter was that his name had been left out.

"The fact of the matter is that you are no longer required to attend evening study hour. You are *exempt.*"

But what about the problems at the end of Chapter One, which he had been told to leave until today? For some reason this question made the assistant master very angry, and he shut the door in his face.

Aware of his insecure position, Thomas took to scrutinizing the Director's Notice Board several times a day in order not to be caught off guard a second time. But it made no difference, he realized, whether he saw these notices or not, for once they had been displayed on the board they were irrevocable, the matter in question already beyond his control: they were absolute and indisputable decrees. He approached the notice board with feelings almost of dread. Anything might be made the subject of such notices, which appeared mysteriously and without warning. It might be a regulation about leaving shoes in the corridor. But Thomas would not have been a bit surprised to find a notice there stating that the following morning he would be taken out into the yard and shot. It would be there among the other notices about leaving shoes in the corridor or removing cutlery from the dining hall, and it would be in no way distinguishable from these.

Perhaps such feelings could partly be explained by his unfamiliarity with the way things were done at the Home, but there was a much more immediate reason. His dread of the notice board had to do with the acute discomfort he felt at seeing his own name written and displayed for everyone to see, exacerbated by an act which, although understandable, had been rather foolish, and for which he had only himself to blame: he had secretly removed the notice referring to himself.

A couple of days after the first notice had gone up he discovered a second. To anyone else it must have appeared quite harmless.

Redecoration of the sick bay. —From 8 a.m. tomorrow morning until further notice the sick bay will be *out of bounds* owing to redecoration and maintenance work.

Thomas puzzled over this notice. On the one hand it seemed unnecessary to tell people not to go where they had no intention of going in any case. And on the other, the notice ignored what was for him the relevant point: the sick bay was where he slept. How could the room in which he slept be put out of bounds, apparently with no thought for where else he was to sleep? It was the first he'd heard of the matter.

The Matron was very offhand when he asked her about it. Something or other would turn up, she said vaguely, but she was too busy to deal with it now. She told him to come back in an hour.

One hour later Matron was just as busy. She didn't seem at all pleased to see him.

"I don't know what it is," she said crossly, "but you manage to make more trouble than all the rest of them put together."

She told him to go and have a look at the box room on the landing below the attic.

The box room was not really a room, however, but a sort of very tall cupboard, stuffed up to the ceiling with suitcases, lampshades and nondescript junk. It was out of the question.

"Couldn't you squeeze a camp bed in somehow?" asked Matron doubtfully. She went to have a look for herself, perhaps just to spite him.

"Well then," she said, "it can't be helped. We'll have to put you up on a camp bed in the dormitory. It's only for now."

Thomas was sure she was right. The significance of what

had been happening over the last few days was only too plain. He was being given to understand that there was no space for him at the Home.

It was no doubt in order to confirm this officially that Mr. Girdon had asked to see him in his drawing room at seven o'clock the following evening.

This time Thomas took no chances. Well in advance he found out exactly where the director's private rooms were and how to get there, and he arrived with plenty of time in hand. However, it didn't seem that he was expected. Far from it. From the chink of glasses and rumbling laughter he could hear as he stood waiting outside the door it sounded very much as if Mr. Girdon was giving a party.

After he had been waiting for about a quarter of an hour the door opened and a man with a reddish face, obviously drunk, came stumbling out. He looked at Thomas in astonishment.

"What are you doing here?"

"Waiting to see Mr. Girdon. . . ."

"Waiting to—amazing!"

The man stuck his head back round the door and called out.

"Mr. Girdon sir! Mr. Girdon—"

There was so much noise in the room that he had difficulty in making himself heard.

"Mr. Girdon, sir! Boy here. Astonishing boy. Says he wants to see you. Do you want to see *him?*"

"Oh, that," came Mr. Girdon's voice. "Forgot all about it. We'd better have him in."

"Where's the lavatory?"

"Opposite."

The man with the reddish face lurched across the corridor. Thomas went in.

It was very warm in the room. No doubt for this reason the windows stood wide open and the men had drawn up their chairs to benefit from the coolness of the terrace. Apart from the man with the reddish face who had just gone to the lavatory, three men had gathered in the director's drawing room, all with their backs to the door. Consequently they did not see Thomas come in, and as nobody gave any sign of wanting to take notice of him he decided to keep in the background until a suitable opportunity presented itself. He looked around for a chair to sit on, but all he could find was an uncomfortable stool by the wall.

The man with whom Mr. Girdon was engaged in animated conversation somehow seemed familiar, and Thomas suddenly realized that it was the welfare officer, of course. The assistant master was also there, apparently fast asleep.

"When you consider the question of *identity*," Mr. Girdon was saying, standing with his back to Thomas and rising alarmingly off the balls of his feet whenever he emphasized a word, "you must also bear in mind the question of *continuity*. There are two factors, natural and cultural, which guarantee continuity: biological heredity and external tradition. We locate identity at the point of intersection of these two factors. Tradition or, *for our purposes*, memory has a function not unlike heredity. Just as memory incorporates past experience in our perception of the present, so tradition is subsumed under the continuing development of a culture. However . . ."

The man with the reddish face came back into the room carrying a bottle, and proceeded to fill all their glasses.

"The weak point here, it seems to me, lies in the ready assumption of a continuity of external tradition, of culture itself. For if this is not assumed, and I do not think it can be, the implications in respect of identity are somewhat disturbing. The same interdependent relations, I should like to suggest, subsist between identity and culture as between an organism and its environment. Culture is as inescapably a part, an exten-

———

7 3

sion of identity as is the environment of an organism. A culture characterized by discontinuity and by inference instability, a culture we should like to define by its increasingly abrupt cycles of innovation and obsolescence—no no, *not* criticize, my dear fellow, for that would be quite absurd—must surely effect corresponding changes in people's sense of identity, possibly in our notion of identity *per se.* Well now, I rather think it does. And the change it effects is really not at all unlike losing one's memory."

"Which brings us back to the point," began the welfare officer.

"Exactly!" said the red-faced man with unexpected ferocity. He stood facing them, a little unsteady on his feet, his hands thrust into his pockets.

The welfare officer ignored the interruption.

"About the examination results—"

"You will find them in the envelope on the table in front of you, but you needn't bother to look. I can tell you what you'll find—nothing. Not one answer, you see, not a single one. Not even attempted. Naturally I take a serious view of the matter, and a still more serious view of the fact that for at least part of the examination he had simply absconded. But that need not concern us here. Nor need it concern us whether I, or you, or anybody else takes a serious view of the matter. It doesn't make a scrap of difference whether we do or not. *It is much bigger than that.* The boy is completely ignorant. But even if he were a bit less ignorant, would that make anything better? A bit more, a bit less, quite a bit more, quite a bit less—really, it makes no odds. For when one considers all that there is, theoretically, to be known, or the very least that one might be required to know, even quite a bit more is still *infinitesimal.* And this is the point. You see what I mean?"

There was something disturbingly familiar about these words, and perhaps that was why, although Thomas had understood almost nothing, he found the tone of what Mr. Girdon was saying extremely sinister. The director's words reminded him of the evening of his arrival at the Home. And then it suddenly became clear to him that of course Mr. Girdon was *perfectly well aware of him sitting there,* and the fact that he chose to speak with his back turned toward him as if he had forgotten about his existence was every bit as important as what he was actually saying.

"There is a sense in which a person cannot see an environment he doesn't know. And further, there is a sense in which an environment he does not know does not effectively exist either."

Mr. Girdon waited, as if he were anticipating a question, or perhaps in order to let his words sink in.

"Because he is ignorant, you see. He looks blindly at the world around him. Combustion, electricity, molecule, atom, integrated circuits, relativity . . . he knows these words, after a fashion, but not what they signify. The forces they represent are registered merely in certain impulses and sensations of which he is bodily aware; a rudimentary physical awareness, nothing more. The sense faculties with which he experiences the world, these crude instruments he has dragged unchanged from the paleolithic age into a world of the most arcane and subtle constructions, batten merely on immediate surface happenings, without an inkling of what is at the base. His picture is fragmentary. And worse, it is misleading. The vital information he requires for a fuller, more accurate perception of what is the case must increasingly be supplied by other than his sense faculties. The information he does receive through his senses must in turn be used selectively. A lot of it has to be discounted. It is merely noise, interference, reflecting that huge redundant volume of sensations involuntarily thrust on him. So he has had to learn to do two things, to suppress a lot of information that is naturally forthcoming and to supply a lot more that isn't there. He does this all the time. Obviously his perception has come to function in a different way. What has happened? In order to be effective he must be able to repudiate a very natural part of himself: what his senses are telling him. And so the dissociation of sense from perception begins. His new mode of perception is characterized by the dichotomy of a tangible world sensually perceived and an intangible world known by purely formal ratiocinative process. Surely this sense-knowledge dichotomy of perception will modify his relation to his environment. There is a loss in immediacy. Imperceptibly it leads to the estrangement of the subject from what he perceives. Surely there are withdrawal pains, for the spirit, when he repudiates a natural part of himself. Estrangement, indifference, listlessness, atrophy, torpor. Accidie."

The director stood up, cracking his knuckles with a flourish.

"Accidie—"

At this point he was interrupted by a spluttering sound from the man with the reddish face. He wanted to say something, but was unable to get it out. At first Thomas thought he must have choked; then, to his amazement, he realized that the man was laughing. His foot jerked out with a curious sideways, spasmodic movement, and he clutched the table so violently that the glasses began to rattle, waking the assistant master up. He began to laugh out loud. Mr. Girdon looked puzzled for a moment, and then his face broke unexpectedly into a grin. Perhaps there was something funny in what he had said, and the others also suddenly saw the point which had escaped Thomas, or perhaps they were just stampeded by the tremendous braying peal of laughter: within a few seconds all four of them had begun to laugh and the room was in complete uproar. Thomas had the sensation of being trapped in a room that had suddenly begun to flood with appalling speed.

———

After what seemed a very long time the laughter subsided. The red-faced man got unsteadily to his feet and wandered over to a pile of golf clubs that were stacked in a corner of the room. Mr. Girdon said something in an undertone to the welfare officer, which Thomas did not catch, and not what the welfare officer said in reply either, for just at this moment the red-faced man started rummaging noisily through the pile of golf clubs. He finally extracted a putter and went out onto the terrace, but as a result of this interruption Thomas missed what had obviously been a vital piece of information.

"How far does a thing have to change to become another? When two or three people are born with a missing limb they are called mutants; but whenever larger numbers of people are born with what is thought of as a defect, what are the consequences to be drawn? One redefines the human body. As if this condition were some kind of obscure disease, something you could treat people for. Wrong. It's not a personal, but a generic condition. Not an aberration, but an indication of evolutionary change, already well established and requiring to be judged by new standards. You see what I mean? So what are the consequences to be drawn? Well, I would rather think that one must begin to redefine what is meant by a human being."

From outside came the sound of a golf ball being gently putted across the lawn.

"By the way, could you manage a round of golf on Saturday?"

"By all means. . . ."

As the two men moved towards the terrace Thomas hesitantly came forward, hoping there would now be an opportunity to discuss his case: why he had not been consulted about his clothes being removed from his suitcase, why he had been moved out to the scullery for his meals, why he no longer had a proper bed to sleep in, and all those many shadowy questions which seemed, so unjustly, to hang on such a slender thread—his failure in the examination.

But when he tried to make all this clear Mr. Girdon only looked at him with a mixture of incomprehension and amazement.

"Discuss your case? But it already has been discussed. What do you suppose we've been doing for the past half hour?"

Thomas was at a complete loss.

"Pack your bags, dear boy! Hurry! It's all been settled. You're leaving with the welfare officer in ten minutes."

It was in these peculiar circumstances that Thomas N. left the Home and went to live in an approved boardinghouse, by chance only a mile or so from the place where he had been found over two months before.

Towards eleven o'clock one eve-
ning, in pouring rain, Thomas walked up the steps of the house
in Long Street and took the front-door key out of his pocket.
The lights were on as usual in the ground-floor rooms overlooking the street and in one room on the second floor. The rooms
on the first floor were dark. Inserting the key into the lock, he
glanced across at the bay window of the room on the right and
saw, as he was expecting, a very slight movement of the curtain,
so slight that it could have been hooked over no more than the
tip of a little finger, as someone unseen, but who he knew must
be standing just behind the curtain, let it fall. There was no
mystery about it: it was his landlady, looking out to see who
was coming into the house.

He ferried softly across the dark hall and started up the
stairs, quietly but very fast, two and three steps at a time. There
wasn't a sound in the house. Just as he was turning at the
second flight of stairs he caught sight, again as expected, although he never heard any door open, of a sudden fissure of
light lunging across the floor of the hall below. He hurried over
the landing, went into his room and locked the door behind
him.

He had walked back through the rain without a coat. It
had been raining for most of the day, but when he went out he
had forgotten to close the window. He stood and watched the
rain rebounding from the window ledge; a fine whiskery spray
had pitted the floor in a semicircle beneath the window. Closing

---

it reluctantly, he took off his shirt and trousers, hung them over the back of the chair and switched on the fire. The next five minutes he spent carefully examining the room for traces that anything had been disturbed. He had done this every evening since his arrival at the boardinghouse two weeks before.

"This is the young man," the welfare officer had said, introducing him to the landlady of the approved boardinghouse.

She had a hard face which looked as if it had been polished. She put on her glasses in order to look at him better, and said, "I see. All right," but Thomas wasn't sure what this referred to.

"I expect he'll want to see the room."

Something about the way she said this caused the welfare officer to become extremely apologetic. She paid no attention, however, and led the way upstairs. Thomas followed her. He noticed her tight skirt and black shoes with silver buckles, sharp and a little threatening, like spurs. Without a word she opened the door and stood aside for him to see the room. Thomas asked her about a cactus that was standing on the shelf.

"There'll be an extra charge for the cactus, if you want it," she said, but that wasn't what he meant. He followed her back downstairs in silence.

A large, very plain girl appeared mysteriously and made them some tea. She spoke to nobody and nobody spoke to her. For some reason the atmosphere seemed a little tense. After a while the welfare officer turned to Thomas and said that he and the landlady had business to discuss, so he went up and sat in the room. For better or worse it was now his room, as a result of a simple transaction involving a slim brown envelope which the welfare officer had handed the landlady, by way of identification he had first thought, the moment they stepped into the house.

Their discussion went on for almost an hour. After the

―――――

welfare officer had left, the landlady called him into the room where they had had tea and shut the door.

"There are a couple of things I'd like to get straight from the start. This is a quiet house, and I want to keep it that way. Mr. Peters, my husband, is an invalid. His condition makes him sensitive to the slightest noise. That's why he lives at the top of the house, to be disturbed as little as possible. Poor man, he's practically confined to his room, so—well, I'm sure you'll sympathize and want to cooperate. Until now I've been very lucky with my lodgers. The other gentleman, of course, is hardly ever in, so that causes no problems. You leave us in peace and we'll leave you in peace. That's the first thing. And then there's my daughter Lisa. I don't want to have you interfering with her."

She came over to the table where he was sitting and stubbed out her cigarette vehemently.

"Not in any way. Understand?"

"Yes."

She sniffed, and quite unexpectedly began dabbing her eyes with a tiny handkerchief which Thomas had not seen her take out, but which she must have conjured out of her sleeve.

"I'm sorry, I didn't mean it to sound like that. But if you knew what I've been through with that girl. God knows, if I hadn't stood by her I don't like to *think* where she'd be now."

She looked down at the floor, as if ashamed of what she was about to confide.

"When we were having tea, she was in here for a moment, you'll have noticed it straightaway."

Thomas had to admit that he hadn't actually been struck by anything in particular. Of course the girl was very plain, but that was probably not what his landlady meant.

"My daughter is backward. What they call retarded. Her mind never fully developed."

She raised her eyes and looked directly at him. Perhaps it was her intention in some way to appeal to him with this look, but the impression Thomas got was quite different. He instinctively felt that his landlady was an extremely cold woman.

"Sometimes she'll seem quite normal. She fools a lot of people. Mr. Peters and I are the only ones who *really* know. There's no question of her going out and earning her living and leading an ordinary life like any other young girl. She just wouldn't be able to cope. On the other hand her case isn't bad enough to warrant putting her away in a home, even if I had the heart. It's neither one thing nor the other with her. But believe me, that's the least of my troubles."

She paused to light another cigarette.

"I expect you're wondering why I'm telling you all this. Well, it's because I want to warn you to be on your guard. From now on you're going to be living in this house, one of the family, so to speak, so you might as well find out sooner rather than later. It's a terrible thing for a mother to have to say about her own daughter, but there it is—I'm afraid Lisa's not what people call a very nice sort of girl. It may be through no fault of her own. I don't know. She's certainly had a decent upbringing. Sometimes I think I can see her father in her—I don't mean Mr. Peters. He's my second husband. My first husband was a thoroughly bad sort. Where else can she have got it from? Lying and stealing and putting about nasty little stories. Nasty's not the word for it. Disgusting and obscene. I've had lodgers in the past, it was all I could do to prevent them from going to the police. I had to go down on my hands and knees. I'm warning you, it'll be no different with you. Never leave the house without locking your door! Before you're halfway down the street she'll be up there taking anything she can lay her hands on. She'll pester you and try to make you listen to her filthy little stories. Take my advice. Ignore her. Don't ever speak to her. Behave as if she didn't exist."

She threw her cigarette into the fireplace.

Since this disturbing conversation on the evening of his arrival two weeks ago Thomas had not seen his landlady once.

The welfare officer had found him a job as a scullery assistant in a large old-fashioned hotel. Considering he had no qualifications, he said, this was as good a position as he was likely to find, and apparently it had prospects. He could work his way up, and perhaps one day find himself the general manager. Thomas took his word for it. There was no alternative in any case. For the time being, any prospects beyond the clatter and sweat of the cramped, stifling kitchens where he washed dishes would obviously remain very remote indeed.

How long Lisa had been spying on him he couldn't say. It was only in the second week that he became aware of it.

When he got back at night the landlady's daughter would stand in the doorway of her room, watching him go up the stairs. He might not have noticed it if the light in the hall had not happened to be out one evening and he was forced to make his way up in darkness. A shaft of light from a door soundlessly opened behind him caused Thomas to look around. He saw the girl standing in the doorway, watching him. She didn't move or give any kind of sign. She just watched him. He didn't know what to make of it. He was about to raise his hand, by way of greeting or whatever, when he remembered that this was exactly what his landlady had been talking about, so he just turned around and went on upstairs.

The same thing happened the next evening, and the evening after that as well. He began climbing the stairs a lot faster to avoid seeing her at all. But the situation made him feel uncomfortable, and this was no longer a feeling he could shrug off lightly, not since a much simpler explanation for the girl's odd behavior, perhaps even (if it was true) for those other things her mother said she did, had suddenly slid into his mind: that in fact she was very lonely. It must have been she who had repeatedly turned out the light, and what happened after, it was all her purpose, to cause him to turn around and notice her as he went up the stairs.

For the first ten days at Long Street Thomas saw no one apart from Lisa. Gradually the house, the peculiar density of its stillness, began to grow oppressive.

Her husband, Mrs. Peters had said, was an invalid, and she had not overstated the case. For all the signs of life that Thomas saw or heard from the floor above Mr. Peters might equally well have been a corpse. The family kept irregular hours. Mr. Peters didn't appear to keep any at all. He never came down himself, but always had other people come up to him. It was never more than one person. Thomas had no way of telling whether it was the same person who went up every day or different people on different days.

But one morning he had been woken by a crash and the sound of something thumping against his door. He got up and looked out. Lisa was sitting at the bottom of the stairs rocking to and fro, holding her head and moaning. The things from the breakfast tray she'd dropped lay scattered over the landing.

"Are you all right?"

He squatted down and touched her shoulder.

"Did you hurt yourself? You must have given your head a nasty bang."

The girl went on rocking to and fro, moaning in a low voice, crooning to herself. Thomas picked up the bits and pieces and put them back on the tray. The girl gradually became quiet.

"At least nothing's broken, and that's lucky."

"Not broken?"

She stopped rocking to and fro and looked up. It was the first time he had heard her speak. Her voice was deep and rather pleasant.

She got to her feet, perhaps too quickly; she swayed and had to lean back against the wall to steady herself. She stood resting against the wall, her head in her hands, uttering little

---

whimpering sounds, rather like a frightened animal. For some reason these sounds irritated him.

"Dizzy," she said. "It's all spinning."

"Perhaps you'd better come and sit down."

"Yes."

He took her into his room and sat her down at the end of the bed. She sat there with a blank, dazed face, absently twisting the buttons on her dressing gown. Thomas watched her in silence. She hadn't washed, her hair was uncombed. Her features were crowded untidily into her face, as if in its making there'd been too little time, as if something had brushed up against it while still moist from her birth and permanently smudged it.

"Are you all right now?" he asked again after a while.

"All right," repeated the girl. She seemed to need to repeat what he said in order not to lose track of it.

"You're very nice to me."

"Well, after all, you're very nice to your stepfather too. You take him his breakfast every morning, don't you."

The girl said nothing.

"You look after him, don't you."

"I'm not supposed to talk about that."

"Not supposed to talk about what?"

"No."

"Why not?"

The girl sucked her lip and said nothing.

"Did you fall down the stairs?"

"I tripped."

She bent forward and held up the hem of her dressing gown with both hands, exposing her thighs.

"It's too long."

"Surprising he didn't hear you fall. Perhaps he did hear you, only he couldn't come out because he's an invalid. Your stepfather's an invalid, isn't he?"

"He's mostly in bed, he's lazy," said the girl carelessly.

"Your mother said he's an invalid."

"He's not really ill. He just pretends he is. But there's nothing the matter with him."

The girl stated this without interest, as a simple fact.

"But if there's nothing the matter with him he must want to get out sometimes."

"Very seldom."

"How long's he been living like that?"

"Years."

"Years!" echoed Thomas.

"Ever since we came here, only it's got more so recently."

"How long have you been living here then?"

She thought for a moment, counting the fingers on both hands.

"Six, seven . . . eight years. My father left when I was eleven. We were just lodgers then."

"Left? Where did he go?"

"I don't know. He just left. That was when Mother started being nice to Mr. Peters. She was very nice to him then."

Thomas nodded.

"Exactly. That's why Mr. Peters married her, isn't it? He wanted her to look after him, because he's an invalid."

"That's not the real reason."

"What's the real reason?"

"He wanted *me* to look after him."

Thomas didn't understand this.

"That was the condition," said the girl slowly. "He didn't really want to marry her. It was she who wanted to marry him. He'd got the house, and money. Mother was always talking about money. That's why she wanted to marry Mr. Peters. He agreed, but on one condition. He wanted me to look after him."

"What d'you mean, he wanted you to look after him?"

"Wash him. Clean his room. Take things up and down. Whatever he needs."

"But why does he want you to do that? Why not your mother?"

"It's not only that," said the girl nervously. "He likes me doing the other things too. But you mustn't let anyone know I told you or I'll get into terrible trouble. Mother pretends not to know about it, but she does. That was the condition when he married her, and she agreed, didn't she?"

"What other things?" persisted Thomas.

"The things that men like you to do," said the girl, becoming more and more agitated. "He likes me to do all sorts of things. Sometimes he strokes me too, and I get into bed and lie under him."

Thomas was stupefied.

"But he's your stepfather."

"Yes, he's mine," said the girl simply.

"And you let him do whatever he wants? Do you *like* it?"

Her brow furrowed.

"I don't know."

"You don't know?"

"Sometimes he's nice to me, because he wants me. Mother doesn't want me. She says she can't stand the sight of me. When she brings people home she tells me to stay in my room. I'm a disgrace to her, she says. She's always brought men home with her, different men."

But Thomas wasn't listening to this.

"D'you mean you sleep with your stepfather?"

"Yes, he sleeps with me," said the girl, nodding her head vigorously. "But please don't tell anybody I told you so. I'd get into terrible trouble."

"He sleeps with you? Your mother knows? And she doesn't do anything to stop it?"

"I've already told you, haven't I?" said the girl fretfully. "It was his condition when he married her."

She fidgeted uneasily and started twisting her buttons again.

"I'd better go. I ought not to be in here."

"Condition? What are you talking about?"

"It's a condition, nobody can change it," whimpered the girl, with a sort of dumb, miserable obstinacy.

"Don't be so stupid! Condition! What does that mean!"

He went over and shook her angrily.

"You don't want to change it, that's how it is! Or perhaps you're making it all up, lying, just as your mother said you would!"

But his getting angry like that hadn't helped them a bit. The girl was just scared and ran away.

He would have liked to talk the matter over with somebody, but the only person he could think of was the lodger in the room across the landing.

"The other gentleman is hardly ever in," Mrs. Peters had said, and she wasn't far wrong—he was never in. But on a Sunday morning he was sure to be at home, and after a lot of hesitation Thomas finally made up his mind to ask him to come out and have lunch with him. So he went across the landing and knocked softly at the door. There was no reply. He knocked again, louder.

He had felt very depressed. Unable to succeed even at simple things like the lodger being in his room on Sunday, he went out to have lunch alone, and otherwise he had sat upstairs looking out of the window, thinking of Lisa and listening for the sound of somebody on the stairs. So the time passed. But by the end of the day, when he could push it out no further, the accumulated desolation of these empty hours returned like an unexpected inrushing tide and remorselessly pulled him under. He felt like a person who knew he was going to drown and that there was no help for it.

But something happened which changed all that. Suddenly things began to pick up pace.

Just as he had been about to go to bed that Sunday night he heard the front door open and close. Somebody came rapidly up the stairs. There was the sound of a key turning in a lock. Without consciously thinking that here at last was the mysterious lodger, without actually knowing what he wanted at all, Thomas snatched open the door and tumbled onto the landing.

The person who was about to step into the room immediately whirled around and let out an exclamation.

"Who the devil are you!"

He was taken aback by the ferocity in the man's voice.

"The new lodger," he said cautiously.

"New lodger? I didn't know there was a new lodger."

He looked at Thomas suspiciously.

"How long have you been here?"

"Almost two weeks."

"Two weeks . . ."

The man appeared to relax a little.

"Well now, there's no objection to that."

This struck him as rather an odd remark. In fact the man struck him as being altogether a rather odd fellow. He had a dense, stocky figure with stooping shoulders, as if the amount of space available for his body were not quite enough. Thomas had been waiting for him to straighten up, until he realized that he never would: he was deformed.

"But what d'you mean by jumping out like that?"

The man stepped back onto the landing and stood with his hands in his pockets, head thrust forward, looking curiously at him. Water dripped steadily from the brim of his hat and his broad black coat. There seemed to be something wrong with his eyes, with how they were set in his face. Maybe this effect was due to the refraction of the very thick lenses of his glasses.

Suddenly he muttered something and darted forward. It was astonishing how quickly he could move. He stopped about a yard in front of him and peered into his face.

"Well!"

After scrutinizing him for a minute he said again:

"Well! But don't worry about me. I'm just a bit short-sighted, you see."

And taking off his sodden floppy hat he twisted it until the last drop of water had been wrung out. He had thick wrists and powerful hands. The way he twisted the hat reminded Thomas of the way a man might wring the neck of a chicken.

He seemed to be much more relaxed now.

"You gave me a bit of a shock, you know, jumping out like that. Almost as if you'd been waiting for me."

He shook out the hat and beat it against his coat.

"Were you waiting for me?"

"Yes, perhaps."

"That's very interesting," he said, beginning to unbutton his coat. "Go on."

"It doesn't matter. It wasn't important."

"Of course it matters. Of course it's important. Look, perhaps we could have a drink."

He darted off and came back with a bottle. They sat down in Thomas' room. The man drank out of the bottle, as he had only one glass, which he insisted on Thomas using. The drink was rather strong, but it had a pleasant warming effect.

The man took a piece of newspaper out of his pocket and read aloud, " 'Who knows mystery boy?' "

He folded the newspaper and put it back in his pocket.

"I've read about you in the papers, you see. It's an interesting case. An extremely interesting case!"

He took a swig from the bottle.

"And you remember nothing? You can tell me nothing about the events before you were picked up by the police?"

The man struck a match and blew it out.

"Where does the flame of a match go to? Ha? Where does the past go to? But that's neither here nor there, is it? To begin with we must establish useful analogies. To begin with I shall call you Kaspar."

"Kaspar?"

"Kaspar Hauser lived a long time ago, about a hundred and fifty years ago. He was a boy of about your age. And like you he came from nowhere, you see. He showed up one day in a provincial town, dressed in rags and hardly able to speak. But he carried a letter with him, which had been written by his former keeper. It was a very strange letter. The writer explained he had kept Kaspar Hauser in absolute secrecy for the past dozen years, and now that his duty was done he was sending him back again. This letter tallied with the account Kaspar later gave of himself, when he had learned to talk properly. He claimed he had spent his entire life in a mud hovel. During all that time he had eaten nothing but bread and water and had never had any company other than a toy wooden horse. He never went outside the hovel. The window was boarded up and let in only a few chinks of light, so he had spent his whole life in darkness. Food and water were brought to the hovel at night, when he was asleep. Whoever brought him the food must have cleaned out his mess and changed his straw. This had been his life for as long as he could remember. But one day a man came to the hovel and told him that the time had come to take him into the world. They traveled during the night and rested during the day. When Kaspar could no longer walk his keeper carried him. In this way they at last reached the gates of a town, where the man set Kaspar down and told him to go on alone. He gave him the letter and disappeared. That was the last Kaspar saw of him."

Thomas stirred uneasily.

"How could his keeper bring him food and water every night without ever being seen? How could he change his straw without waking him?"

"Ah! That's the point," said the man, blinking rapidly and beginning to tap his knee, "that's the point where the newspaper report of the boy called Thomas reminded me of Kaspar Hauser's case: opium. The evidence suggests that his keeper drugged him with opium. How else are we to explain Kaspar's obsession with the taste of water, his insistence that water had ceased to taste like water? What do you think, Kaspar?"

"Did he say that?"

Thomas began to tremble. He was feeling very cold.

"Did his keeper put something in his water?"

The man shrugged.

"It's a possibility. We must work our way back, Kaspar. You must tell me how you came to be sitting here this evening, everything that has happened in the couple of months since you were found on that bench by the river. And beyond, over to the other side of memory. For you have brought things with you from the other side, haven't you. A photograph. A suitcase. You will have to tell me everything!"

The man got very excited. He insisted that it was impossible for a person to completely lose his memory and still be able to function normally otherwise. He seemed to know all about difficult subjects like medicine and neurology, and he explained to Thomas why it was impossible.

"But perhaps it's not memory that's the problem. Perhaps you have lost your way in time."

"What?"

"There is the possibility you have moved sideways in time. Perhaps you are both here and somewhere else simultaneously. . . ."

He had all sorts of methods and ideas, much too complicated for Thomas to follow, but that didn't matter, because he was going to have to work on them first in any case. It all sounded very encouraging. But then the man had suddenly fallen asleep.

It had been impossible to wake him, either, however much he shook him. He must have been very tired, thought Thomas, stretching out on the bed. The next thing he knew it was already light outside and the man was shaking him by the shoulder.

"Thomas!"

"What?" He sat up at once. "What is it?"

"So that *is* your name. I wanted to be sure. Did I talk in my sleep?"

"No. Why?"

"You're sure of that? Well, it doesn't matter. By the way, my name is Onko."

"Onko?"

"That's right. I'll explain later. Come to the bar at the bottom of the road at seven o'clock on Saturday evening. I may have something for you. But don't be late, Kaspar! I won't have much time—"

After that first meeting several days ago the mysterious lodger dropped out of sight again as suddenly as he had appeared. In the meantime Thomas thought about all the things he had said and waited for their next meeting with increasing excitement. He also thought about that bulge he had felt on the man's leg when he shook his ankle and tried to wake him. It seemed an odd place to be carrying a knife, even more odd that a man like him should have been carrying a knife at all.

He must have caught a cold on his way home that evening, for he slept badly and was feverish all night. He slept and woke and fell asleep again, in fits and starts, until well into the morning. At some time during this uneasy interchange of wake and sleep he looked up with surprise to see Lisa, not in the doorway of the room downstairs where he was used to seeing her but just beside his bed, with unfamiliar loosened hair—long, astonishingly long, almost down to her waist; and otherwise naked, standing perfectly still. So he put out his hand and pressed the bluish hollow under her thighbone, and then the bone itself, where the skin was tighter and had a gleam which he somehow thought he ought to put out. There was no putting it out, however. Both the hollow and the bone were wonderfully cool and dry to his touch. If it is real it won't all be like that, he thought to himself: hair for instance will have a different feel, hair between thumb and finger has a gritty, spliced feel like rope made out of gravel. So his hand slid up behind her buttocks into the small of her back, and this was a very peculiar sensation, as if he had eyes in the tips of his fingers looking up to see rope ends hanging down from a belfry—it was hair, of course, with just that feel he'd expected. But then he'd keeled over and gone back under into a heavy sleep, and when he next woke the room was flush with yellow and white light and of course there was no sign of Lisa.

He got up and opened the window. There was no trace

———

95

of the rain last night either. Yesterday had gone away forever, but it must have been there; his shirt still hung over the back of the chair. Now the day outside was bright and hot.

"It's twelve o'clock already. Time to be getting on." He had the whole weekend free. There were quite a lot of chores to be done.

But when he had washed and came back to get dressed he started to shiver and was feeling very queer. This seemed a pity, with that big easy day sprawling outside the window, but there was no help for it. He went to bed again and slept solidly for several hours.

He woke in the middle of the afternoon, feeling much refreshed and extremely hungry. He got up and dressed quickly.

On his way out he realized the door of his room had not been locked. Had he unlocked the door when he went out to wash a couple of hours before? Or had it been unlocked all night? He couldn't remember for sure, and of course it was rather important.

"For if the door had been locked, then naturally there'd be no question of it—she couldn't have got in here and she couldn't have been standing by the bed either. There'd be no doubt about it, that it must have been a dream."

He was unable to get his thoughts clear. It seemed to him at first to be either one thing or the other: if the door had not been locked she must have been in there and it was not a dream. Stupidly he began to grasp that this wasn't necessarily the case.

"Even if the door was not locked it doesn't mean she was in the room." And putting the matter forcibly out of his mind he made his way down into the street.

It was extremely hot outside, not a breath of wind. He began to sweat at once. The standing air felt close and matted, as if it were thickened with the heat and had begun to curdle. He had the sensation of wading through it. Heat waves shimmered above the pavement, receding, always in the same distance. He no longer felt hungry. Perhaps it would have been better to stay indoors after all.

A bus stopped and he got on. It didn't much matter where he went. Sitting at the window he would at least feel cool.

He noticed the girl as soon as he got on the bus. He couldn't very well not have noticed her, because she was the only passenger and the moment he set eyes on her it was clear that there was something different about her. She sat up at the front, her feet on the rail, turning from side to side and laughing, as if she had two invisible companions sitting on either side of her who were taking turns whispering jokes into her ear.

He sat down on the seat opposite. His first impression was of a rather ugly girl. Either her head was too big or her body too small. At any rate, the one didn't belong to the other, and it seemed likely there was quite a bit of argument between the two. Her body was snug and tight but the face was solemn, with precise and severe features that reminded him of the markings on the face of his landlady's clock. She had no shoes on and her toenails were painted bright green.

"Hello," said the girl as soon as she noticed him. "How nice to see you!"

This came out so naturally that there was no doubt she meant it, as if he were exactly the person she'd been waiting to see.

"At least you and I've managed not to get wet," she said gleefully.

"Wet? Why should anybody be wet?"

He asked this quite matter-of-factly, for although it wasn't clear what the girl meant by this remark he was confident she had good reasons for making it.

However, she didn't seem to be in any hurry to answer his question, and perhaps she hadn't even heard it. She stretched up out of her seat, on tiptoe somehow, although she remained sitting, and peered out of the window with an expression of huge delight.

"Such an improvement, turning all the streets into rivers," said the strange girl, becoming stranger every time she opened her mouth. "And so simple! Why on earth didn't they think of it before?"

She turned to him, letting her arm dangle over the back of the seat; like a pendulum, he thought. The corners of her blouse were knotted under her breast, and her bare midriff was dotted with clusters of little golden stars. He saw something fall to the floor. It must have been a star that had fallen. He bent down and dabbed it with his finger.

"Here, one of your stars has come off," he said, holding it out on the tip of his finger.

"Oh, they're always coming off. Never mind. Now what was I saying?"

"Rivers?"

"Yes! D'you know, kingfishers have already been sighted in the center of town," the girl went on in her bright, pebbly voice, "and have you heard that the council are planting willows in all the roundabouts? Just around the corner here, at the top of the street, they're constructing a weir. Can you imagine it? It'll take a while to get things sorted out, I expect. The water traffic on the rivers won't be as heavy as it used to be on the roads, but still. The locks that'll have to be built, the bridges, think of it all! Pedestrian walks over the rooftops, with floating jetties anchored at the windows for public transport ferries to moor. The parks will be flooded, won't they, and turned into bird sanctuaries. Wildlife must be preserved. Salmon will swim up the estuary to spawn in the streets, beaver litter in the submerged aisles of churches and herons roost in the pulpits. Just think of it!"

He was still wondering what to make of this curious

speech when the girl announced in her imperious way that it was time for them to get off, taking it for granted that he would follow, which he did; partly out of curiosity, and partly because in view of what she'd been saying it seemed more likely she would fall off and break her neck. She very nearly did. Misjudging the step down from the bus she ended up slap on her back on the pavement, which to her annoyance turned out to be unexpectedly hard.

He thought the fall would shake her back to her senses, but she said triumphantly:

"You see! That's exactly what I mean. Things can't go on like this for much longer."

He hoisted her to her feet and for a minute they rested in the shade. The girl didn't seem to notice how hot it was. She was so unsteady on her legs that she couldn't have walked more than a dozen yards by herself, but she wanted to get on at once. At least she knew what direction to go in, and to begin with they managed well enough. Then they had to go over a road. The girl refused to cross it. Far too dangerous, she said, anxiously pulling him back from the curb. Thomas was baffled. It was a quiet street with no traffic, but she wouldn't go over on any account.

"It's too deep," she confided at last, "and I can't swim."

So she still hadn't let go of this crazy idea. For her it was not a road but a river; she poured scorn on him for being so blind and stupid. They stood on the corner arguing.

But what if she's right, wondered Thomas. So at last he told her to put her toe over the edge of the curb and see how cold the water was. She admitted that it wasn't really all that cold. He thought it might not be all that deep either, and if the worst came to the worst he thought he could probably swim in any case, so maybe it wouldn't harm to try wading over. Walking out slowly, he reached the middle of the road and reassured her that as it was no more than knee-deep there was nothing to prevent her coming over too. This convinced her. Cautiously she followed him over.

At the next street they turned right and walked down until they reached a dilapidated house with a bright red front door. Outside the house stood a pickup truck with a battered tarpaulin cover rolled back over the frame. House and truck looked as if they might be partners in the same line of business.

"Great Pardoe lives here," said the girl, pushing open a gate in the railings. Thomas only just managed to prevent her from falling into Pardoe's basement.

She hammered on the door. After a few minutes it opened just a crack, revealing a scruffy figure who was unmistakably the third partner in the house and truck business. He looked at them without pleasure.

"It's you, is it. Who's he?"

"Now for Christ's sake don't fuss. He's all right."

Pardoe opened the door reluctantly and allowed them into a dark interior that smelled strongly of fish and oil, giving advance notice of what Thomas had somehow expected: two cats sitting on a heavy piece of machinery at the end of the passage. They were hardly inside when the girl put her arms around Pardoe's neck and started kissing him passionately. He didn't respond at all.

"She's here," said Pardoe after a while.

"Is she now! What a *nice* surprise."

"I'll just go up and get it."

Pardoe disappeared upstairs, and the two of them went into a room where they found a very beautiful girl sitting in the middle of the floor, sorting a pile of shells into two bowls. She looked up at them uninterestedly, quite some distance, it seemed, from behind her steady blue eyes.

"Where's Pardoe?"

"Where you put him."

And until Pardoe came back that was that.

It was cool in the basement, which was a relief to Thomas, as his head had begun to throb unpleasantly. The shell girl sat with her legs curled under her and continued sorting the pile without interruption. She didn't take the slightest notice of him, or of the other girl either, who perched moodily on a stool in the corner of the room, biting her fingernails. His thoughts began to slide and blur. If the city were flooded it was here the water would most quickly rise, and while he could imagine the shell girl of not quite human beauty sitting with floating hair, sorting her shells, in the watery light of a submerged city, there was no doubt in his mind that the other girl who was very mortal and couldn't swim anyhow would be drowned dead within minutes and seconds, perhaps with Pardoe holding her under.

Then Pardoe came back, carrying a small shiny package.

"I suppose you've got the money with you?"

"I never expected to get anything free from you, did I," said the girl bitterly.

He dropped the package at her feet.

"Go on then, have it, and clear out and don't ever come back."

Pulling a wad of notes out of her pocket she jumped to her feet and tried to stuff them into his mouth. Pardoe grabbed her wrist, knocked the money out of her hand and slapped her very hard across the face. The girl froze, looking at him with an expression of disbelief. A telephone rang in the passage. Pardoe let go of her wrist and went out. Her face crumpled and she began to cry. Meanwhile the girl sitting on the floor went on sorting her shells into the two bowls, steadily, with a brittle snicking sound.

"There's a party," announced Pardoe as he came back into the room. "They want us to come over."

He went over to a table, took a pouch out of the drawer and began to roll a cigarette.

"What time is it then?"

"About six."

"Bit early, isn't it?"

"It's been going on since last night."

But Thomas had the impression it was really the other girl Pardoe was talking to. Pardoe lit the cigarette and went across to her, stepping over the money that was still lying on the floor.

"Come on then, Nancy. Here," he said, gently touching her shoulder. She looked up, and he handed her the cigarette. That was all he said, but it was enough, and he knew it was. He stopped to pick up the money and tossed it casually onto the table.

Nancy stopped crying and inhaled deeply. The round face with the precise features which it had occurred to Thomas one might tell the time by was now tear-stained and puffy and looked rather ridiculous: like a waterlogged clock. She got up and passed the cigarette on to him. He held it between thumb and forefinger as he had seen her do, and after taking a couple of drags offered it to the girl on the floor. She shook her head. Pardoe didn't want any either, so he and Nancy finished it between them. The smoke had a sweetish taste but burned his lungs when he inhaled it, and by the time they all got up to go he was feeling dizzy.

The moment they left the cool basement and surfaced in the humid air of the street above he began to feel even worse. Perhaps this would have been the best opportunity to slip off, since he didn't in the least want to go to a party and he had nothing to do with these people anyhow, but he lacked the energy to make such a decision; it was much easier just to let himself be carried along. Everything seemed to be happening very fast. As soon as he and Nancy had climbed into the back the truck swung out from the curb and raced off down the street with a roar and a terrific jolt that sent him rolling across the floor with a pile of loose scaffolding poles. Nancy sat with her arms hooked behind the struts of the frame, her body whipping up and down like a carpet being shaken out.

Wherever they were going it took a very long time to get there, because Pardoe kept stopping to take on other passengers, and at most of the places where they stopped everyone would get out to have a drink. At the last stop they were joined by two other cars and drove the rest of the way in convoy. Among the dozen people crowded into the back of the truck were several drunks, one or other of whom was always in danger of falling off, and a man carrying a trumpet, who aimed it at pedestrians and cyclists with a terrifying blast. The drunks were a rowdy bunch and they soon got menacing, yelling obscenities at passing cars and hurling beer cans through windows. When one of them got hit over the head with a bottle things turned nasty.

At this point the convoy came to a halt. The trumpeter blew a flourish, at the sound of which an enormous man in his underwear came stumbling out of a house, bellowed something unintelligible and vanished inside again. People piled out of the two cars; the crowd in Pardoe's truck, whooping and baying, jumped down into the street and surged headlong into the house. Inside there was a terrific uproar. The drunks and the trumpeter leading the stampede unexpectedly came up against a solid wall with apparently no way out but up the stairs or back through the door, both of which were out of the question, because the people behind them who could not see what was happening decided there was nothing for it but to shove their way in; and the stairs were jammed by another crowd of people who had come out of the upstairs rooms and for some reason were now trying to get down. Overwhelmed by this sudden invasion and the crush on the stairs some of them panicked, lashing out with their feet, which Pardoe's crowd didn't like at all, so they pulled them down over the banisters and punched

---

them in the face, not hurting them badly, but in the process somebody had his glasses smashed and began screaming he'd got splinters in his eyes, and this screaming was so horrible and different from the other curses and shouts that the people who'd been shoving from behind quickly pulled back into the street.

"Take him out of here, quick! Get him to a doctor!"

"For Christ's sake get out of the way!"

Thomas was jostled aside by a couple of people leading a huddled, terrified figure with his hands covering his face out into the road. Furious arguments started up at once, each side so busy blaming the other that they forgot about the man who was standing out in the road scared out of his wits he was going blind. He went on moaning for help until at last somebody bundled him into a car and drove him off. Pardoe's crowd were held responsible for the accident, but they refused to leave unless personally asked by whoever was giving the party. Nobody seemed to know who the host was, however, let alone where he was, so they stood their ground. The other side had no intention of backing down either, and decided to throw them out. No sooner said than done. A free-for-all broke out.

Thomas was standing at a safe distance watching what was going on when something suddenly occurred to him which at once put everything else out of his mind: he had forgotten to meet Onko. He was supposed to come to the bar at seven, and not to be late because Onko didn't have much time. It was already half past.

How could he possibly have forgotten something so important? It gave him such a jolt that he at once scrambled over the fence and mechanically started walking off down the road, forgetting everything but how to get back to Long Street as fast as possible. He had gone about fifty yards when he heard someone behind him calling.

"Hey! Wait!"

He turned around to see Nancy running unsteadily after him. He stopped, walked back a couple of steps hesitantly, and stopped again.

"Hey wait . . . where are you going?"

She came up to him and put her arms around his waist.

"Where *were* you going?"

"Something important's come up. Goodbye."

"Goodbye? What d'you mean, Goodbye?"

"There's a fellow who's arranged a meeting in a bar, and it's very important," he began, at once realizing the absurdity of what he was saying, as he didn't have the slightest idea where he was at the moment and thus very little hope of finding the way back in time. He was also distracted by Nancy putting her arms more tightly around him, to steady herself or whatever, at any rate a lot tighter, and as a result the sense of urgency he meant to convey was diverted from the words he was saying into much more immediate, localized sensations on his body, unmistakably of her breasts, and an uncontrollable surge of images exploding and spinning like catherine wheels across his mind. Why for goodness sake a belfry? But there was no point in pursuing this further, and besides, she was suggesting they take a taxi, which he accepted gratefully, for it was a much more practical idea and imposed at least a semblance of order on a situation that had clearly got out of hand.

Nancy talked nonstop all the way in the taxi, mostly about a sister who had been run over and drowned a year ago —how could she be run over and drown?—but that was about all he could remember, for his mind was too blurred to pay much attention. Finally, at about eight o'clock, they reached the bar, and Thomas walked through the door just in time to catch sight of Onko banging the table with his fist so violently that he could have sworn the glass of the man sitting opposite him bounced clear of the table by several inches.

———

*T*here was such a lot of noise in the bar anyway that Onko's banging the table didn't seem to attract any attention. Tucking his hands under his armpits, as if to prevent them from doing any more damage, he thrust his head forward and began talking energetically to the man opposite him, oblivious of everything else going on around him. Thomas made his way forward, but instead of going up to Onko he remained standing several yards away, looking around the room as if he had not yet spotted him. And when Nancy asked him if he could see his friend anywhere he found himself telling a quite unnecessary lie. Which is exactly how it begins, he thought uneasily, you think it's nothing at all and suddenly you're in it up to your neck.

Nancy was already installed at the counter, flirting with a couple of men who were buying her drinks, but he didn't realize this because he was standing with his back to her watching Onko and his companion. He drew a little closer to their table. Reluctant to interrupt them, he waited for Onko to look up and recognize him, perhaps ask him to join them—there might still be a chance, although it was already so late. But things seemed to have slipped entirely out of his control. For several minutes he stood there listening to them, becoming increasingly puzzled. They must have been talking, for he could see their lips move, and certainly there was a tremendous din going on in the bar; but that hardly accounted for the very peculiar fact that *he couldn't understand a single word of what they were saying.* It was stifling in the room, and the noise seemed to be getting worse and worse: noise which was somehow stacked in tiers, like crockery, stacked in tiers and mysteriously shattering, tier after tier, shattering. Perhaps he should ask Onko and his friend to speak up a bit so that he could understand what they were saying; and he leaned forward with just that intention when Onko interrupted his friend, picked up their glasses and handed them to somebody with the words "Yes they're dead," at which point Thomas felt something snap inside his head, as if hooking into a ratchet, and he began to feel very stupid indeed. For he realized that all this time Onko and his companion had been speaking a foreign language.

"Now that's a very odd thing," he said aloud to himself, trying the language out. Of course it was something perfectly familiar and commonplace, but he felt it with a sense of marvel, having forgotten how it felt, like a hand taken out of a glove. All these effects, he decided, the not realizing it was a different language they'd been speaking, the crockery shattering in tiers, all these things must be due to the stuff he'd been smoking in Pardoe's basement and the drinks he'd had on the way here. Reassured that he was getting the situation back under control, he leaned forward again and tapped Onko on the shoulder.

Onko swiveled around and half rose out of his chair. He screwed up his eyes and said with a laugh, "Oh it's you," but there was no mistaking the fact that even here in a room full of people he was just as startled as when Thomas had unexpectedly come out onto the landing that evening. Thomas wondered what it was that made him seem on edge all the time. For some reason he didn't look too pleased, so he changed his mind about what he had been meaning to tell him and said instead, "How about coming along to a party," realizing as he said this that he was repeatedly having to glance at Onko's companion because as soon as he looked away he'd forgotten what he looked like. "Party?" inquired Onko, blinking rapidly. "What d'you mean, party?" He grunted and twitched his nostrils, as if he were rolling the word back and forth over the bridge of his nose. Thomas explained what had been happening, without the slightest interest. He hadn't meant to invite Onko to a party, far from it, the two of them had much more important matters to discuss. It was simply the first thing that came into his head. Onko and his companion exchanged a few words, and Onko said sharply, "Are you sure about this girl? Where is she?"

Thomas had completely forgotten about Nancy. He turned around to look for her.

She was standing at the counter, leaning on somebody's shoulder, an empty glass dangling upside down from her hand. The man she was leaning against was in the middle of a sentence, and it must have seemed to him that he'd got her nicely in hand when suddenly she dropped the glass and began to sob. At first she didn't make any sound, nobody seemed to have heard the glass shatter either, so when the man saw her shoulders jerking he patted her on the back and said "Hey!" because he thought she must have swallowed something the wrong way; but realizing after a while that something else was the matter he got a bit alarmed and said "Hey, hey, hey!" three times, in a quite different tone of voice. Thomas heard him say this and he could see what was happening to Nancy, but it was still such an inward, private kind of sobbing that apart from himself and the fellow she was leaning against nobody seemed to notice. The man went on saying "Hey!" and a lot of other meaningless words as fast as he could in an embarrassed undertone, trying in some way to prop her up with the words, or maybe to wall her in and smother her with them instead. "Better get her out of here," Thomas heard someone say, just as Nancy folded up, as if on hinges, simultaneously at the neck, hips and knees. She was like a deck chair folding itself up in slow motion. She collapsed tidily, sitting back on her heels, her arms wrapped tightly around the man's legs. He looked down sheepishly, wondering what to do with the glass he was holding, and he had to do something with it, for he looked very silly with that glass in his hand and the girl sobbing at his feet. He made a few untidy scattering gestures with the other hand and tried to raise his leg, as if wanting to polish his shoes on his trouser leg. "Stick it on her head then," someone called out and everybody began to laugh, the fellow with Nancy at his feet also began laughing, pell-mell, running for cover after a fashion, with the glass bouncing in his hand. Nancy knelt there clasping his legs, her shoulders shaking, and no one doubted that this was because she was laughing too.

Thomas stretched out his little finger and said to Onko: "That's the girl."

"What's she up to? What's the big joke?"

"She's crying, as a matter of fact."

He had the pleasant, languid feeling of watching it all happen through a pane of glass, completely detached.

At last the man was able to dispose of his glass and persuaded Nancy to get up. Thomas saw her look around, apparently searching for him. He told Onko and his friend that he had to be going now, if they wanted to come along they were welcome, and a second later he was out of his chair, effortlessly, with no sense of movement, standing just behind Nancy with one hand cupping her elbow; which was unaccountable, since while he was doing this he had the impression of remaining sitting where he was, looking on from a considerable distance, and in a flash he remembered what Onko had said about being in two places at one time. Nancy chattered away as if nothing had happened. They were all going back to the party, she and her new friends, and if it wasn't any good there they'd move on to her place. Again Thomas had the strange sensation of listening to Nancy explaining that they ought to be getting on their way, and himself thinking that by and by maybe they would, when in fact they were already heading for the door, and it wasn't until they got out onto the street that his awareness of what was happening caught up with what was actually happening, the arresting sight of Nancy standing by the railing spewing a smooth white jet of vomit into someone's garden.

"Amazing she's still on her feet," he heard someone behind him say, and turning around he saw Onko looking on with his hands in his pockets. Somebody unlocked a car and said three of them could get into the back, so he climbed in beside Onko and the friend whose face he could never remember and they drove off after the other car. There was an unpleasant smell in the backseat, of rotting leather he thought at first, until he realized that it came from Onko, perhaps not so much from him as from the jacket he was wearing. Onko talked fluently, unaware of his smell, about his ideas of how to deal with Kaspar's case, but whatever Onko said it was still overpowered by the combination of that extremely unpleasant smell and an image which had stuck fast in Thomas' mind: the image of Onko standing with his hands in his pockets, looking up at someone about to jump off a very high tower.

In no time at all they arrived back at the house, only to find that the party had broken up. A handful of people were sitting out on the steps smoking and talking; the others had left after the police came around to investigate complaints about the disturbance. There'd been another skirmish with the police. A couple of Pardoe's friends had been charged with assault and removed from the premises. A vacant, rather dispirited mood had set in, made worse by the fact that there was nothing left to drink, so Nancy's suggestion that they cut their losses and move on to her place was very welcome. Within a few minutes they were on the road again.

Somehow Thomas lost sight of Onko and found himself packed into another car with five people whom he didn't know. He was squeezed into the corner by a very fat girl who fell asleep the moment she sat down. Another girl was driving. Soon after they started it became clear that one of the men sitting in front beside her was hallucinating badly and ought not to have been let into the car at all. He started rocking backward and forward excitedly, rapping the panel over the dashboard with his knuckles.

"Come on now. C'mon! What're you doing, for Christ's sake? Make this miserable little crate fly! Fly it, for Christ's sake!"

"How do you make it fly then?" asked the girl who was driving, but she wasn't being funny, she could see the state he was in.

"Drive for the lights. Don't be scared. Drive straight for the lights!"

"And then we'll fly?"

"Sure we'll fly. You can go right through those lights, very cleanly, they'll just suck us in, I swear it!"

"And once we're through the lights?"

"Bing! we take off. Airborne, just like that!"

He began jigging around on the seat.

"Faster! Faster!"

Out of the corner of his eye Thomas noticed a slight movement beside him, somebody's hand, reaching over to unbutton the girl's blouse. It was the man on the other side of the girl. He unbuttoned the blouse down to her waist and tried to pull it off her shoulders. The fat girl sat with her head thrown back and her mouth open, breathing evenly. She was fast asleep. The man sat looking out of the window and casually began to squeeze her breasts, almost absentmindedly, as if he had nothing to do with his hand.

The car swerved violently.

"You crazy fucker!"

The fellow in front lunged past the man between himself and the driver and made a grab at the steering wheel. The girl lashed out with her fist and hit him in the face, fortunately waking up the other man beside her just in time to drag him away from the wheel. She must have hit him hard. Blood was streaming from his nose, but he paid no attention, hardly seemed to have felt anything. He started jigging crazily up and down again, yelling at the girl to drive faster and take the car through the lights. The other man kept hold of his wrist, but the girl was anxious he'd fall back asleep, so she kept on digging him with her elbow and asking him questions, anything that came into her head, to keep him awake. All this time the girl beside Thomas slept on, her breasts uncovered, the man on the far side stroking them in silence with his face turned to the window.

Downtown the streets caught fire and became a blaze of lights. The fellow in front went wild. He wanted them to drive up onto the pavement through the crowds. This rattled the girl, and she told the other man to hit him again to keep him away from the wheel, but it made no difference, he went on raving and begging her to drive into the crowds. She had the others get his head down so that he couldn't see; a terrific struggle started up in the front seat. The girl pulled up at the side of the road, shouting at Thomas to get out and open the front door. The three of them forced his head down between his knees, rammed him forward under the panel and twisted his arms up behind his back so that he couldn't move, but he screamed and swore all the rest of the way, and that must have been about half an hour's drive.

The house was a big place, at the end of a dead-end road, set some way back from the street. The others had already arrived. No lights were on in the neighboring houses. It was very quiet. When Thomas got out he noticed a smell of grass and leaves. They pushed through the flower-crowded gate along a path that led around the house. Deep summer scents rose astonishingly up off the garden, drenching the dark. It seemed to Thomas he was walking through a standing haze of scents, not gravel underfoot but crushed flowers. Someone had wandered off into the garden, he could hear his voice, delighted, like a child's, come tinkling out of the dark. He stopped to trail his fingers in the water of a little pool, only for a moment, but when he looked up the others had disappeared. He followed the path to the corner of the house, where a soft light spilled out over a flight of steps that seemed to lead down to the basement. Presumably this was where everyone had gone. He could hear people talking, and he thought he recognized Onko's voice among them.

But when he got down into the basement there was no sign of Onko or of anybody else whom he knew. He found himself standing in the middle of a very large room, asking where Nancy was. Nobody knew. Nobody seemed even to know who she was. For what felt like a very long time he remained standing there, as it were sealed off and disjointed from everything around him, in a terrifying solitude. He wondered if he had come to the wrong house. But of course all these people must have been there before, at the other place. It was just that in the dark and the confusion he had not been able to remember their faces. It could be explained quite easily after all. So he went to look upstairs instead, all three floors, right to the top of the house.

From the stairs he could hear somebody up there having an argument. A door at the end of the landing opened, and framed in the brightness of the room behind her Nancy came unsurprisingly towards him in a long white gown, with shining eyes and rippling strides, drawing a train of light after her down the dark landing.

Someone passed in the doorway of the room beyond. He caught a glimpse of shelves along the walls, and in the shelves what appeared to be dolls.

"Did you come for me? How sweet! Where are the others?"

"Downstairs. —There's somebody in your room."

"How do I look? Aren't you starving? Come on!"

He followed her down, running his finger along the wall. It was covered with silk.

"Surely you don't live here alone?"

"It's my parents' house. But they're hardly ever here."

"So you have all the dolls instead: the dolls keep you company."

Nancy stopped and looked at him anxiously.

"Oh but don't tell anybody that, will you. Please."

Her face was very white. At this rate she won't last long, thought Thomas.

"Can't you be *there* a bit more?"

She frowned and ran her hands all over him, as if she were blind, putting him together with her fingertips.

The next thing he knew they were standing in the big room downstairs, listening to a music that without any doubt was also clearly visible, shaped like a vortex, into which he found himself inescapably drawn, not by anybody, but by the sheer sucking force of the vortical swirl itself, effortlessly folding him in and closing over him. He moved with the music, as thick as blood in its dark sluggish arterial flow, almost lazily towards the heart, but at the center of the vortex the beat became quicker and he found himself bucked and spinning, beyond his control, in tight gyrations, as if he were swinging a team of horses anchored to the palms of his outstretched hands; around and around he saw them snort and plunge, with flying hair and heads toppling, barely astride their bodies, like hobbyhorses on a merry-go-round. Hurtled out of the center he came up smack against Nancy somewhere, stuck fast, and together they went spinning out and away into colossal unlit spaces, a white-hot breakaway star, burning the air, disintegrating, briefly trailing its marvelous plumage of light. There was no feeling, no body, nothing.

When he awoke it was pitch-dark.

It made no difference whether his eyes were open or shut. The dark was so dense and close-grained he seemed to be lying in a shroud, trussed up, from head to foot. It was crammed into his ears, nostrils and mouth, tasting parched, like dry mud.

For a long time he lay without moving. Then he put his hand to his chest.

He touched moisture first, and then skin. He was lying naked, covered in sweat. The heat was intense. The sweat stood on his body like a glaze. The pores were submerged. His body could not breathe.

He sat up, resting on his knuckles. He tried to brush the sweat from his chest and arms, but it was tacky and would not run.

He got up and moved forward till he touched something. It was a wall. The plaster was wonderfully cool.

He followed the wall to the corner, from the corner along the second wall, hand over hand, pushing against the solid vertical dark, until he had been right around the room.

There was no door.

After a while he began to make his way back, cautiously, without hurry. He numbered the corners, saying each number out loud. At the fourth corner he stopped again. His hands rested on the hard, cool plaster. There could be no doubt about that. But there was also no doubt that whichever way around

---

the room he went it made no difference, there was no door, and no window either.

His forehead prickled.

"There must be a door."

Almost as soon as he said it he put out his hand and found he was groping in a space where there was no longer any wall. Taking possession of this space firmly with both hands before it closed up again he stepped quickly forward. The texture of the darkness was now different. It was less dense.

He seemed to be in a passage.

He walked forward gingerly, and as he moved off his heel became aware of a little draft scudding under the sole of his foot. The draft came from the foot of a door, which he could not see, but which he could feel. The door stood slightly ajar. He pushed it open.

Mysteriously there was no light switch, but the floor of the room was tiled, and so he guessed it must be a bathroom. He found the basin and turned on the tap.

He drank and drank.

The water was like a drug. He stretched out on the tiles, which were cool. He could feel them drawing the heat out of his body. The tiles grew warm, and soon his heat was outside him, he was lying on it.

He had no idea how long he lay in the bathroom, and no memory of leaving it.

When he next woke he was lying on his back on a bed. It took a long time to wake, or at least, he had to come up a long way. There was a sense of pressure decreasing, as if he were moving very gradually up a shallow incline from the seabed to the surface.

It took him about as long to wake as it did for the day to become light.

First he registered a loss, a shrinkage of darkness. The dark woof unraveled and shrank before his eyes, like a fabric becoming threadbare. It fell apart. It looked shabby. There was still no sense of light.

As the dark scattered, all traces too of his sleeping intuition of things began fading fast. Out of the shabby, porous dark little beads of light were sweated, with a sense of terrific strain. Very suddenly there was no question of it becoming light. It was light. He was awake and fully conscious.

This waking and becoming conscious was not a coming to but a parting from, deprivation of what had been before. He awoke with a sense of loss. Into the fragile, powdery, grizzled light at break of day he strained his eyes. The blurred sense of loss, blur of things lost which had been apparent to his introverted sleeping eye was recovered and brought into uneasy focus; as a sense, at first, of displacement, and then of appalling premonitory misgiving.

He sat up and waited for the growing of the light. It changed minute by minute. Minute by minute, intuiting beyond what he could see, he assembled the forms of objects, dismantled and recomposed them. During the erratic phase of the light, and later, when it became more concentrated, what these objects were, or what he saw them to be, changed.

By the wall opposite the bed, directly facing him, was a chair. The chair did not change, however. He knew it was a chair from the start. It merely became more palpable.

It was a gaunt kind of chair with a high hooped back and curiously foreshortened legs.

From the subtle configurations of light it appeared that the back of the chair was ribbed out with struts fretted in a sort of wooden filigree. But it had a lack of symmetry that troubled him.

By degrees he realized this might be due to something having been placed on the chair, something that was not a part of the chair.

It was a bundle of clothes, with a pair of stockings, or

---

perhaps trousers, draped over it and hanging down either side in crumpled folds.

He lay back and looked at the ceiling.

The light rose.

He looked at the bundle of clothes. He could see them quite clearly now. He looked at them steadily for a long time, thinking about the clothes, but seeing something different. No sense was to be made of it at all. It wasn't a bundle of clothes on the chair. It was a human head.

There was no question of being mistaken about this. It was Nancy's head.

He lay perfectly still and looked at the head.

The head was severed. It had been cut off the body. The body was not there.

The head had been severed from the body.

It was a severed head on the chair.

He got up and drew the curtains, carefully, without hurry. It was the normal thing to draw the curtains when one got up. Normality, ordinary procedure, must not be lost. He took his time drawing the curtains, observing himself scrupulously, how he did it, and the effects of his doing it. These were exactly as expected. So when he turned back to the severed head he saw it for the first time with a shock. For the head on the chair, and how he saw it, was there in just the same way the windows and the curtains were.

He began to look at the casual objects around him in the room with a terrifyingly urgent, sharpened sense of their being there. The severed head was one of these objects, and like the others it was at the same time both terrifying and casual.

The head was tilted forward. The eyes, open and stark, stared at the floor. Matted strands of hair stuck to the forehead and temples. The mouth was twisted, the lips slightly parted.

All the horror and deadness of the face was in the slumped, rigid jaw. Around the face the hair fell down in staggered folds, as if it had frozen.

Beneath the chair her blood had stained the carpet in an uneven trellised pattern. The seat of the chair was perforated. The individual spots of blood were regularly spaced, but directly underneath the head they were much darker; the blood funneling from the neck, it was natural the drip had been stronger there. Blood was all over the chair. It had spilled from the rim of the seat and down the legs. In some places it was still tacky, like fresh candle wax.

There were blood spatterings on the wall behind the chair. The head might have been swung by the hair when it was lifted onto the chair, flicking drops against the wall. Between the chair and the door there were barely any stains.

The door was leaned to. He drew it open and went out into the corridor.

There had been terrible carnage here.

She must have been beheaded a few yards down the corridor, just outside the next room. The carpet had been battered and plowed up. It was sluiced with blood, great pools, gaping like holes. The walls were streaked and slashed. Tufts of carpet, splinters, gristle and pieces of flesh lay shredded around a spot on the floor where several huge gashes had torn open the carpet, exposing the floorboards. The head had been struck off here. Little bloodied drippings, felt and flesh, not identifiable, had spurted up and stuck to the walls.

It looked as if the head had rolled a yard or two. There was a curious oily smear, whose texture was thicker and darker than blood, tracing an unsteady arc from the spot where the head had been severed to where it might have lain, perhaps for minutes, in a pool of its own blood. Why were the head and body in different rooms?

He saw the body when he looked up through the open door of the next room.

It had been tossed onto a heap of dolls and toys in the corner where it lay sprawled, completely naked, in a very strange posture.

One leg was bent at the knee, splayed out away from the hip. The exposed sole was dirty. The other leg was stretched out straight. From the pit of the belly to the navel the skin was smudged and discolored, as if dusted with charcoal. When he went closer he saw that the hair between her legs was shriveled. Apparently it had been singed. The body buckled at the hips and sagged inwards. The left hand lay in the space where there was no head, somehow quite naturally, as though she were resting her wrist on her forehead. The right arm was flung up behind her, outstretched, the knuckles just touching the wall. Her fist was clenched. In her hand was the stub of a burnt candle.

The limbs and torso of the corpse seemed to lie quietly, with scarcely any trace of violence. But the upper part of the trunk, between the shoulders, had been trenched open, leaving a bloodied mangle of burst skin and splintered bone. One shattered end of the collarbone stuck out.

On the floor her white robe lay where it had fallen, as if she had just stepped out of it.

He picked it up. It was spotless.

Overcome by an urgent need to relieve himself he stumbled down the corridor into the bathroom and defecated. The feces were tight and odorless. At the basin he washed and drank. Stooping to drink, he remembered he had drunk there before. He remembered the room which had seemed to have no door. Had she already been dead then? What had happened?

Straightening up, he had a tremendous shock. He saw his face in a mirror above the basin.

His face was covered with blood.

———

There was blood all over his throat and chest.

There was blood on the insides of his wrists. It was on his shoulders and down the backs of his arms. His fingers and fingernails were bloody.

"It can't be blood. It's not possible."

But he was aware of the blood on his face, he could put his hand there and touch it; and for this there was an exact correspondence in the mirror, impersonal and outside him, where he could see his hand touching the blood he was aware of.

He panicked.

He completely lost control.

Feeling wetness on the inside of his leg, he looked down and saw that he had squirted urine over himself.

He squatted on the bathroom floor and hugged his knees and started rocking to and fro.

"What about the room? There can't be a room without a door. And if there were, it wouldn't be possible to walk out of it. So either way, it can't have been there."

This idea seemed to hold out a certain hope.

He got up at once and went back into the corridor. It led out onto the passage landing and the stairs down to the next floor. For some minutes he stood at the top of the stairs, listening. There was not a sound in the house.

The first room, with the shelves of dolls, was visible from the outside landing. He could remember having seen it the night before. This was where the body of the girl was now lying. Next was the bedroom. He had woken there. The head was on a chair opposite the bed, separated by about ten or fifteen feet from the body in the adjacent room. Across the corridor were the lavatory and bathroom; also a kitchen, which he had not noticed before. Opposite the kitchen was one further room.

He went into this room. The floor was carpeted, but

otherwise it was empty and undecorated. Along the base of the walls there were curious niches, about six inches deep and two feet high. The room also had a fifth wall.

The fifth wall extended from the doorway about two yards into the room, like a fixed screen, although it did not appear to be a screen. It was only a few inches thick, but very solid. Holes had been bored on the inside of this wall, and brackets attached. There were corresponding fixtures on the parallel wall. Apart from a large skylight there were no windows.

It slowly became clear to him what must have happened. He had started from the corner to the left of the doorway, passed around the room anticlockwise and then back again, thinking he had returned to the corner from which he had started. He had mistaken the corner formed by the short screen wall for the corner to the left of the doorway. If he had kept on going around the same way instead of turning back, in fact if he had started from almost any other point in the room, he would have found the doorway without difficulty. However, the fact of the matter was that he had started from this point and not any other. That was how it had happened.

"So that's how it happened," he said aloud.

For a long time he just stood there, with this obstinate fact of the fifth wall heavy in his mind. Either way the room can't be there. But absurdly enough it was there, with its enabling fifth wall. He was standing in it. He stared at the wall in disbelief, as if it had played a stupendous trick on him. For there was no doubt as to the conclusion that must be drawn: something he had been quite sure about, which he had ruled out as categorically impossible, could in fact very easily be the case.

"This is what comes of overlooking things. Things mustn't be overlooked! Always keep on the alert. Act now!"

The muscles stood up in his stomach. He made a tremendous effort and went out into the corridor.

The situation had suddenly become different. It was a fact that he had blood all over him. Through the bedroom door he looked at the head on the chair. Looking at the chair, he was aware of the blood on himself. In fact he no longer really looked at the head. He was already accustomed to it. He was thinking of somebody coming through the door at any moment and seeing him there with the blood on him.

Obviously the blood would have to be washed off.

He went into the bathroom and turned on the taps. While the water was running he stood at the basin, scrubbing his hands with a nailbrush. He turned and turned each hand, looking carefully between the fingers. His fingers and hands had so many tiny crevices and wrinkles; the blood seemed to be in every one of them. It had lodged under his fingernails.

"Don't overlook the fingernails."

He scrubbed until the tips of his fingers felt like bristles.

When the bath was full he turned off the taps and got into the water. The blood came off easily. The water colored. He stood up and looked over his shoulder in the mirror, at his neck, his back, the insides of his arms. It was all clean. He let the water run out and then he cleaned the bath too.

He looked out of the window and saw to his alarm that the sun was already very high. Hours had passed. He must get out of the house as fast as possible.

After a search he eventually found his clothes on the bedroom floor.

To his dismay there were bloodstains on the trouser bottoms. Examining all his clothes carefully he discovered spots of blood on the shirt collar too. It was inexplicable that there was blood on his shirt; it had lain under the trousers.

He went into the kitchen and hunted through the drawers for a pair of scissors. Spreading the trousers out on the floor, he squatted down and began to cut off the trouser legs about four inches from the bottom. The scissors were blunt. It was a laborious job.

It was getting very warm in the kitchen. He opened the window.

When he was satisfied that the trousers had no other marks on them he got dressed. He decided it would be better to risk leaving the spots of blood on his shirt, since it might attract unnecessary attention if he were to cut off the collar.

He went into the bedroom to fetch his shoes. However, he couldn't put his shoes on because the laces were knotted, so he sat down on the bed with the shoes and set about unknotting the laces. Little obstacles like this caused panic to flare up inside him. It took several minutes to get the knots undone. When he stood up to put his shoes on he realized he had been sitting there all that time and had completely forgotten about the head on the chair beside him.

Surely it ought to be possible to go now. He would have a last look in each of the rooms, one by one.

But it wasn't as easy as that. In the bathroom he noticed the floor was still wet. There seemed to be faint pinkish smears on its wetness. So he took a rag and rubbed the floor till it shone, and when he had also rubbed the basin and the tiles on the outside of the bath he carefully washed out the rag several times.

Instead of feeling better for all this activity he knew he had made things much worse. The implications of having made a start in the first place with this business of cleaning up gradually dawned on him. He was no longer just cleaning up. He had begun to cover up.

He resisted this idea.

"Of course there's no question of anything being covered up."

He knew perfectly well that the first thing to be done when he left the house was to go to the nearest police station and report the murder.

However, when he glanced in the mirror over the basin there was no denying that there were really quite a lot more stains on his collar than he had at first realized. He had already cut off the ends of his trousers. Perhaps that was a mistake. He'd been a bit hasty. But once the trouser ends had been cut off there was no possible way of getting them back on again. No possible way. It had to be one thing or the other.

There was something just as final about the ends that had been cut off the trousers as about the head that had been cut off the body.

He went back into the kitchen, took off his shirt and cut out the collar. The collar and trouser ends lay on the floor. Either one thing or the other. He couldn't leave them anywhere in the apartment. They would have to go with him. So he picked them up and put them in his pockets. He made up his mind not to let what he had done with the shirt collar and the trouser ends in any way influence his handling of the situation as a whole. Mentally he put them on one side. They didn't count.

He started at the end of the corridor, taking the easiest room first. The room with the fifth wall had nothing in it. That was perfectly straightforward.

Next he went into the kitchen. The scissors had to be washed. He replaced them in the drawer. That was all here. He closed the kitchen door.

The bathroom had been done already. He flushed the lavatory once more. The floor was dry now. There was nothing to indicate that anyone had been in there at all.

He went into the bedroom. Nothing could be done about the head. But what about the bed? Would it be better to make the bed, or to leave it unmade?

———

He made the bed, and then finding that this looked unnatural unmade it again. Somehow he couldn't get clear of the bed. He looked under it, he lifted the mattress, he shook out the sheets. It was not a question of looking for something, he told himself, but of overlooking something. A little pink handkerchief fell out of the folds of the sheets. Presumably it was hers. But he didn't find anything else.

"In any case, what would you expect to find?"

Nonetheless, he had another look under the bed. It took an immense effort to be able to leave the room.

He stood in the corridor looking at the headless body on the pile of dolls.

"There's not much that can be done about that."

He looked into all the rooms once more, very quickly, just to reassure himself.

Eventually Thomas left the apartment.

Going downstairs was like going back into a world which he had been out of for a very long time. He passed a clock on the stairs. It was already midday.

The house was still. He made his way warily along the basement passage into the big room. It was littered with wreckage. The bar in the corner had been overturned. Bottles and glasses were smashed, fittings torn from the walls. But he hardly noticed this. He walked straight through the room and out of the door, shading his eyes as he emerged at the top of the steps. Outside the garden buzzed and hummed in the bright sunlight.

Closing the gate behind him he came out into the street. A man was out there washing his car. Thomas walked past him. The man did not look up. At the end of the street he turned left into the main road. He quickened his pace.

After walking for a few minutes he found a shop open.

———

He went into the shop and asked to be directed to the nearest police station. The shopkeeper asked him if there was anything the matter. He said there was nothing the matter. The shopkeeper came out into the road and started pointing and explaining how to get to the police station. While he was listening to the shopkeeper's directions it occurred to him that it would be a great deal simpler to tell the shopkeeper what had happened and ask him to telephone the police. But by this time the shopkeeper had finished explaining how to get there and was hurrying back into the shop to serve a customer, so he might as well get around there and report the matter himself.

It took him about ten minutes to reach the police station. It was a large building, much larger than he had somehow expected. There were pillars on either side of the entrance. He was disconcerted by these pillars. For a couple of minutes he stood indecisively on the pavement, looking up at the pillars and the unexpected largeness of the building. His heart began to beat faster.

"Of course it would be easier without the pillars. It would be easier if the building were smaller."

He walked on a hundred yards or so and then stopped again.

"But after all, what difference do the pillars make? What does it matter if the building is large? It doesn't change anything."

While this resolution was still strong in his mind he walked back down the street and without pausing went straight into the building.

Between the street and the inside of the police station there was nothing but a door, but Thomas was nonetheless astonished to find how quickly he had passed through that door and was now inescapably inside. He had thought it would somehow take much longer to get into the building. He found himself in a big hall with a high ceiling and checkered stone floor. On one side a polished wooden counter stretched across the hall. A man was leaning against this counter talking to a policeman who stood opposite him typing. The counter was divided off into partitions. Above each of these partitions hung a sign, which Thomas did not have time to read, however, because the moment he entered a second policeman came into view and advanced slowly from the back of the room, frowning slightly, sliding his index finger between his neck and the collar of his shirt. He stood at the counter impassively, waiting for Thomas to come up to him. Something about this man, the way he stood there waiting with his finger inserted into his collar, at once convinced Thomas that he was not the right man to talk to about such an urgent matter, and so when he said "Yes?" in an inquiring tone of voice Thomas jerked his head and pointed in the direction of his colleague who stood typing at the end of the counter. The sign hanging there read: "Lost and Found." The policeman shrugged and moved on down to the other end, where he leisurely began sorting a bundle of files. Thomas sat down on a bench by the wall with a thumping heart.

It can't be done straight out like that, it needs time, he said to himself. He could hear the policeman riffling the pages of the files at the far end of the counter, but he looked at the floor in order to avoid catching his eye.

After a while he felt his heart gradually beginning to beat less fast. He rubbed his palms along his thighs. There is time now, he thought, and when the man here has finished, after that, it will be quite easy. For a minute he rested. He felt quite composed. It would be easy after all. But then he noticed his ragged trousers, and he had to rub his palms a second time along his thighs, and to his dismay he became aware of a terrific sweat standing out on his forehead. This is ridiculous, it is cool in here. If it is cool in here there is no reason to sweat; and there is no other reason either. But you cannot be in a cool place and sweat and talk about these things at the same time. Naturally they will ask: Why does he sweat? He comes in here to report a murder, and he sweats, although it is cool. The sweat must be rubbed off. He hastily pulled out his handkerchief. With the handkerchief out came the bloodstained shirt collar too and before he could catch it, it fell to the floor.

Just as the shirt collar fell to the floor the man at the counter said, "All right then," and turned away, Thomas picked up the collar, the policeman said something like "Yesse" and he hurriedly got to his feet—suddenly with no more time, disabled by the awareness of the collar he was holding under the counter. So instead of saying what he had come in there to say he asked the way to the nearest station, but not wanting the other policeman at the end of the counter to hear what he was saying, since it might arouse his suspicions, he spoke so softly that the man opposite him could not hear him either and asked him to repeat what he had said. There was nothing for it. Thomas blurted out the first thing that came into his head.

"Has a key ring been handed in here this morning?"

He was asked to describe the key ring, which he did with great facility, offering a detailed account of the circumstances in which it had been lost, how there was a hole in his pocket, and so on, whatever occurred to him. A check was made. No, nothing of that description had been handed in. The policeman was most helpful. Thomas thanked him for his trouble and went out.

When he was back in the street he realized for the first time what a beautiful morning it was.

"Well, no key ring has been found, nothing of that description," he said aloud to himself. He felt exhausted but relieved, as if his terrible ordeal were now well and truly behind him.

After all, the murder of the girl had nothing to do with him. It was not his business.

He set off home.

The girl's body was found by the cleaning lady. She notified the local police, and within an hour of their arrival at the house a murder investigation had got under way.

Apart from a skylight in one room at the top of the house no windows were open; after an unbroken spell of hot summer weather the flesh of the head and corpse had very rapidly begun to decompose. Swarms of flies, like a festering collar, browsed and flickered at the base of the neck and crawled in and out of the orifices of the putrefying body. Over this wreckage, no longer quite human, the fetid air hung in the rooms like a rotting shroud.

The outstanding feature of the crime was its savagery. It was not a killing; it was butchery. The victim's life had been torn out of her, her body destroyed and taken apart with the same fury and brutish violence that had vandalized the rooms in the basement of the house. Her murderer or murderers had gone far beyond the requirements of any rational motive. The decapitation of the corpse and the terrific gouges in the floorboards also indicated considerable physical strength. The head had been severed with probably not more than three or four blows; remarkably, since the instrument with which the blows had been struck appeared to have had a rather blunt edge. The skin tissue had been not so much cut as broken by sheer force.

The curious position of the head and trunk and their distribution in different rooms could be variously interpreted,

---

but in view of evidence that the victim had been abused the arrangement of the corpse must have been deliberate. Traces of wax were found in the pubic region and on the thighs; discoloration of the abdominal skin was superficial, caused by the light scorching of an open flame, the candle, presumably, which the victim held clutched in her right hand. That she might accidentally have spilled wax over herself was feasible, but under no conceivable circumstances could she have wanted to burn herself. What had been done to her with the burning candle had definitely been done by someone else.

Whether or not it had been the intention of that person to mock his victim, his draping her over the pile of dolls could only have been done for a deliberate effect, displaying a casualness, a ghoulish indifference to the monstrousness of the deed itself which it was difficult to reconcile with the spontaneous, uncontrollable actions, as at first sight they appeared, of a killer who had gone berserk.

Matters were complicated by evidence that a large number of people had been present in the house at about the time the murder occurred. It was quite feasible that the damage done to property, the decapitation and the subsequent abuse of the victim were the responsibility of different persons or groups of persons acting together at the same time or independently at different times. Until the autopsy had established the approximate time of death, and this had been compared with forensic evidence relating to the rate of decay of food samples and similar exhibits, it was impossible to say whether the girl had been murdered at the same time these persons were in her house, or some time after or even, theoretically, before.

The house had not been broken into. There were no indications of forced entry, and the cleaning lady confirmed that nothing was missing. In her experience it often happened that the girl didn't bother to lock up the house, and during the warm weather they had been having recently she might have left doors and windows open even when she was out of the house, so anybody could easily have got into the house at any time.

But with what intention would persons unknown to the girl want to get into the house if not to take something from it? Why would they have caused so much unnecessary damage, presumably making a lot of noise and risking detection? And why kill her? It seemed much more likely that the girl knew these persons, that perhaps they were her guests and had come to the house for a party at her own invitation.

The cleaning lady identified the victim as Nancy Julia Fleming, aged nineteen. She had just completed her first year at art college. Her parents owned the house but were apparently very seldom there as the father had extensive business interests which frequently took him abroad. His wife usually accompanied him. Financially the girl was well cared for, but the relationship with the parents did not appear to have been a good one.

The corpse was removed from the house during the course of the afternoon, and for the next few days forensic experts continued their examination of the premises. The parents of the deceased had gone on holiday, leaving no address. It was a week before the police were able to notify them of what had happened.

The murder of Nancy Fleming caused a sensation, attracting considerable public interest over a period of several months.

A certain prurience undoubtedly fed that interest, but the barbarousness of the crime deeply shocked the general public. In a civilized country a personable young girl from an affluent background had been done to death, decapitated and horribly abused in her own home, apparently by someone she had herself invited there. Worse still, there did not appear to be any motive. Perhaps the deeper roots of the public outrage lay less in the fact that such an appalling crime offended against all the standards of behavior in a civilized society than in an uneasy suspicion that, on the contrary, it might rather be taken as representative of them.

This disturbing absence of motive was compounded by the failure of the police to identify a single person with any connection to the crime. They had now established that on the night the girl was murdered a party had been held in her house which at least fifteen people had attended. Why could none of them be traced? And why, despite police appeals and extensive press coverage, had none of them come forward voluntarily either?

When the police leaked details of forensic analysis showing that drugs had been used it at once led to new speculations in the press. A drug orgy had led to the bloodbath; the victim had been hacked to death by drug fiends. Finding traces of drugs on the premises was one thing, proving that the girl had also been murdered by a person under their influence was quite another, but in most reports of the case this was freely assumed. There were good reasons for this assumption: it disposed of the question of motive.

The discovery of drugs at the house seemed to explain why no witnesses had come forward—fear of prosecution, not merely on drug charges, but for murder. Assuming that most of the guests at the party had taken drugs, the notion of collective guilt, actual or implicit, was not one that could easily be dismissed. Their reluctance might also be due to their not having any clear recollection of what had actually happened that night. Perhaps some of them would not remember having been there at all.

In addition to that, it was quite possible that many of the guests had not met the murdered girl before the evening in question, did not know her name, and would not recognize the pictures of Nancy Fleming published in the newspapers—the last ones available were a year old and bore little resemblance to her.

A young police officer by the name of Havel was assigned to the case. From the start of the investigations he had been unimpressed by attempts to explain the evidence as pointing to a group murder, and despite the appearances he doubted it had been carried out by someone who, for whatever reason, had been out of his senses. Arriving at the house that Monday morning and taking stock of the scene of the crime for the first time, he was struck by his own very powerful feeling that the victim had been murdered in cold blood.

It was a serious discrepancy, he thought, and not merely an accident, that the traces of a large number of people in a confined space should on the one hand be so apparent and still, on the other, be insufficient to make it possible to identify any of them. Supposedly a group of people had come to the house for a party, under the influence of drugs they had turned into a frenzied mob rampaging through the house, smashing up property and finally murdering a girl in what must have been an orgy of blood—and then they had mysteriously vanished from the premises without a single piece of personal evidence, a handkerchief or a button, having been left behind as proof that they were there.

Havel's doubts were reinforced by another very puzzling discrepancy concerning the incidence of fingerprints in the house. There was no lack of prints, and many of them were very clear; but whereas in the basement just about everything had been touched, and not merely by one person but several, in the apartment at the top of the house no fingerprints were to be found anywhere except on certain personal objects, belonging to the victim, which had been handled by her alone. On door handles, for example, and other surfaces where one might expect to find prints, if not of other people then at least of the murdered girl, no traces could be identified. He drew the obvious conclusion. All these surfaces must have been wiped.

Why had these surfaces been wiped in the apartment where the murder had taken place, but not in the rooms downstairs where the party had been held? In the event that a group of people who had attended the party were responsible for the murder, and had been sufficiently clearheaded to take the precaution afterwards of wiping all the surfaces they had touched in the apartment upstairs, surely they would also have done this downstairs; and in the event that they were so far beyond control of themselves as to be unconscious of what they had done then they would not have thought of wiping out any fingerprints at all.

Even if one assumed, as Havel was inclined to, that a single person had murdered the girl and had done so coldbloodedly, it was hard to explain this discrepancy. Was this person one of the guests who had eaten and drunk with the other guests downstairs before going up and murdering the girl, someone so sure that he had not touched anything there that he hadn't bothered to take the same precautions downstairs which he had taken upstairs? He could only be sure of it if he had been constantly mindful of it, and in that case it was inexplicable that when he went upstairs later he had touched so many surfaces on which he might have left fingerprints that he had found it necessary to wipe them all.

From changes in the activity of alkali phosphates in the area of the vital wound the pathologist estimated that death had occurred about a week before the corpse was discovered. He was unable to be more specific owing to the length of time the subject had already been dead and the unusually warm conditions in which the corpse had lain.

Apart from the severance of the vertebral column at the neck, the immediate cause of death, the victim did not appear to have sustained any other injuries. He deduced that the wounds had been inflicted with a quite small instrument, such as a chopper or meat cleaver, which had not been particularly sharp. The head had been separated from the trunk with not more than five blows. Considering the type of instrument used, the operation had been done with remarkable efficiency, requiring both strength and skill.

Some time before her death the subject had taken a quite large quantity of lysergic acid diethylamide.

Analysis of food and other organic matter found in the basement suggested that the victim had died at approximately the time a party had been held at her house. Otherwise examination of the premises yielded meager results. No trace of the murder weapon was found.

Routine neighborhood inquiries established that only one person had been struck by anything unusual on the weekend in question. One of the residents in the street had returned home at about one o'clock on the Sunday morning to find several vehicles parked in front of the Flemings' house. Nobody had seen cars parked outside the house later that day, and nobody could remember having seen anybody leaving the house. So no persons had actually been seen or heard at all, neither coming nor going.

Nancy Fleming turned out to be just as elusive a person as the circumstances of her death were mysterious. Her parents were rich, so she lived in a rich neighborhood, but she had no contact with the other residents. They had met the girl but did not know her personally, and they tended to judge her by the company she kept—unpleasant, scruffy characters, as one resident put it, who would turn up at the house at all hours of the night. The neighbors blamed the girl's parents for what had happened.

Havel's own interview with the parents when they came over for the funeral was disappointing. There had been another daughter, two years older than Nancy, of whom they had apparently been much fonder. She had died in a car accident six months previously. Nancy was very attached to her sister and had been badly affected by her death. The parents didn't like the idea of Nancy living alone in the house and had wanted to let it, but she was a stubborn, self-willed girl, they said, and they had been unable to persuade her to move elsewhere.

The information they were able to give Havel about their daughter was useless, since they were so clearly out of touch with what had actually been going on. They were astonished to hear about the change in her life-style, the company she had been keeping and the sinister world of drugs in which she had recently moved. "If only I'd known!" the mother repeatedly told Havel. She was a vain, stupid woman. Havel guessed that mother and daughter had long since become strangers.

Inquiries at the art school Nancy had been attending for the past year were not much more helpful. Her attendance had been irregular and she had not mixed with the other students. Nobody could say much about her private life; she went with a different set. However, there had been a striking deterioration in her appearance over the past few months and apparently this was due to her reckless use of drugs, which several students had known about.

But the very dearth of information about Nancy after her death gave Havel a picture of what her life must have been like. Had an obituary been required she left no friends, or none that were traceable, who would have been able to write it.

It struck Havel as being a characteristically modern type of murder. The girl had lived alone in a big city, moving in an obscure floating world of casual encounters, and in much the same way she looked for her pleasure she had met her death, at the brief, wholly fortuitous congruence of people and events that had little more in common than the accident of their coming together.

At the edge of this wasteland all the tracks the investigation had been following seemed to peter out, but just as things were at their bleakest Havel had a stroke of luck: a set of fingerprints which the police already had on their files. The fingerprints were those of John James Pardoe, unemployed, who had been convicted of larceny and given a suspended sentence three years previously.

The case had been out of the newspapers for a couple of days when this unexpected breakthrough again made the headlines. Man detained in Fleming case; first lead in headless girl case. Large quantities of cannabis resin and LSD were found in Pardoe's house. He was arrested on charges of possession of drugs.

The police had not expected to find drugs in the house. At their last encounter Pardoe had been self-employed in the scrap-metal trade. His branching out into a new line of business, as a narcotics dealer, maintaining his previous connections in the scrap trade merely as a cover, was unknown to them. Havel assumed that the drugs used at the party that night were provided by Pardoe, and that he had been supplying Nancy as a regular customer for some time past. In connection with a murder case this could turn out to be an extremely serious charge. Even if drugs could not be shown to have any direct bearing on the case there remained aspects of moral complicity whose implications in a court of law were not lost on Pardoe.

He denied ever having supplied Nancy with drugs. He said he had met her for the first time about a year and a half ago, and for a while they lived together. The relationship didn't work out too well, however, and after a year they had gradually drifted apart. Perhaps he'd drifted a bit more than she had. At that time he'd met his current girlfriend. Nancy was extremely jealous. Their relationship broke up six months ago.

Quite unexpectedly Nancy had turned up at his house that Saturday afternoon. Why had she come? He couldn't say why, she had just turned up. He'd not seen anything of her for over two months. There had been somebody with her. He could remember nothing about this person other than that he had seemed to be very young. How young? Perhaps about seventeen or so. Surely he could give them some idea of what this person looked like? Pardoe said he was the sort of person one didn't notice. He didn't know his name either. He couldn't remember anybody even having spoken to him.

In the late afternoon they'd set off to a friend's house for a party. They'd stopped to pick up a number of people on the way—quite a lot of people, friends and their friends, whom he didn't know. Did any of these people know Nancy? He couldn't say.

As soon as they got to the party he lost sight of Nancy for several hours. The next time he saw her was about eleven o'clock, when she'd invited everybody to come around to her house.

How many people had gone on to Nancy's house? Pardoe said he'd given about a dozen people a lift in his truck, and there were several other cars as well. He had seen Nancy getting into one of these cars. Maybe the others had followed, or maybe she'd given them the address. Did that mean that everybody who'd been at the first house also went over to Nancy's place? Quite a lot of people had left early, he said, but anybody still at the house at around eleven o'clock probably did. He also remembered that on the way to Nancy's house he'd been asked to stop so that somebody could get out. A man. The incident stuck in his mind because if he hadn't shouted at the man as he was crossing the road he would have walked straight into a car. He had no idea who it was.

What about the person who had come to his house with Nancy? The last time Pardoe could remember having seen him was when he climbed into the back of the truck outside his house. He hadn't seen him at the party, and not at Nancy's place either. It was dark, of course, and there'd been a lot of people.

What had happened at Nancy's house? Well, said Pardoe, the usual sort of thing that happened at parties. It had just been an ordinary party, at any rate for as long as he was there. He and his friends had left at about one-thirty because they wanted to spend Sunday out in the country. Nancy had been alive at the time they left, and a few other people were still in the house. He'd already told them that.

Who did Pardoe think he was kidding? Was it the usual sort of thing at parties for fittings to be ripped from the walls and furniture demolished? What about the girl lying headless upstairs at the end of the evening? How had it come to that? Pardoe had no idea. Several people had got very drunk, and maybe after he'd left they had "gone a bit wild." If drugs had been taken at the party they must have been supplied by Nancy. In that case, of course, anything could have happened. There was no telling what might happen when people went over the top. But he hadn't noticed anything of that sort while he was there. He didn't know anything about it.

The extraordinary difficulty of reconstructing the events of that night became apparent to Havel when he started questioning the growing number of witnesses, contacted through Pardoe's information, who could tell them about anything that had happened at the house. At best their recollections were hazy. Quite a number of them claimed to have woken up the next morning without even being able to remember where they had been or how they had got home. Some of them admitted having been "very drunk," but they all denied having taken drugs and maintained they knew nothing about drugs having been used at the party. Even those who claimed to have a clearer recollection of what had happened were unreliable witnesses. They described objects, for example, which didn't exist in the house. Perhaps they were truthfully reporting their experiences, but evidently these were experiences of a reality already distorted by drugs.

Havel foresaw that what complicated the inquiries into the case of Nancy Fleming would later bedevil the trial: not just the difficulty in ascertaining the truth of the events of that night, but the more subtle paradox that how those events were described might subjectively, perhaps, be true, and at the same time not compatible with how they had actually happened.

There was one witness, however, whose reliability Havel thought dependable. The statement made by Pardoe's girlfriend, independently of Pardoe's own evidence, corroborated what he had said in almost every detail. What gave it particular weight was the fact that she appeared to have been the only person to have left the party completely sober. She also remembered and was able to describe the person who had come to the house with Nancy early on Saturday afternoon. This was important, as it was apparently the same person who figured in the evidence given by a number of other people.

An impression based on this description was published in the national newspapers, and the following day the police received an anonymous telephone call suggesting that it bore a striking likeness to a photograph which had appeared in a local paper a couple of months before. The police compared the two pictures. There was not an obvious likeness, but Havel was much more interested in the fact that they already had a file on this person mentioning both drugs and a history of mental illness.

The feeling of relief that had come over Thomas when he left the police station that Sunday afternoon lasted only as far as Long Street. When he actually turned into the street and was in sight of the house he began to have serious misgivings. He stopped and debated whether he should turn back. The feeling that he ought to turn back was very strong, but as it was not quite clear where he should go back to he changed his mind again and walked on.

Perhaps it was this little uncertainty just before he reached the house, coupled with his dislike of the landlady's habit of spying on him, that prompted him to go around by the alley at the back instead of using the front steps as he usually did. It was not as if he thought of taking any kind of precaution, at least, not deliberately so; but on the other hand maybe that was exactly what he had in mind. At any rate, it was a most unfortunate decision, for he had no sooner slipped into the house through the back door than he ran straight into Mrs. Peters crossing the hall in her underwear with a skirt folded over her arm and a flatiron in her hand.

"What on earth d'you think you're doing?" she asked sharply.

"Nothing."

"Nothing? What does that mean? I thought I particularly asked you not to come in the back way. D'you think I've got a team of servants to clean up after you whenever you come in?"

"No," said Thomas. He tried to avoid looking directly at Mrs. Peters and found himself staring at her garter belt instead, which made him even more confused. She noticed his confusion, and she guessed the reason.

"Have you only just got back?"

He said nothing.

"Look at you! Don't think I don't know what you've been up to! The welfare officer looked in this morning to see you and wasn't at all pleased to find you weren't in. He'll want an explanation, you mark my words!"

She marched into her room and shut the door.

Upstairs he found two notes pinned to his door, one of them from Onko and the other from the welfare officer. The note from Onko had been there since half past six that morning; it said that he had left early because he was going away on holiday and would not be back for a couple of weeks.

The other note was very brief.

"Sunday, 11 a.m. Came around to see you as arranged, but you were not in. Call me back as soon as possible."

The unexpected appearance of these notes on his door worried Thomas. He felt as if he had been caught off guard.

"But off what guard?"

He hurried into his room, and as he changed out of his tattered shirt and trousers considered what to do. Why did the welfare officer have to come around today of all days? "As arranged," it said in the note, but he couldn't remember any such arrangement. He cursed his luck. What made things worse was that the welfare officer must also have seen Onko's note, and from that it would seem he hadn't been back to Long Street at all that night. Why did Onko have to write such a careless note? Why write the time on it? Why pin it on the door instead of slipping it under the door? For the note certainly made it look very much as if Thomas hadn't been in his room at all that night. And if he hadn't been in his room, where *had* he been?

He dropped his shirt onto the floor and stood stock-still, concentrating as hard as possible. His mind was completely blank. Where the devil had he been then? By some curious trick it was Mrs. Peters' voice he heard asking this question, just as clearly as when she'd been standing downstairs in her garter belt with a flatiron in her hand.

He'd been to a party of course. It was quite straightforward—so what was the problem? Without a moment's delay he hurried off to the phone booth down the street and called the welfare officer's number, but there was no reply.

As he came back into the house Mrs. Peters opened the door of her room and stuck her head out.

"Well, you've read his note I suppose?"

"Yes."

"And what did he have to say?"

"Nothing. He wasn't in."

Obviously his landlady had read the note.

Feeling very uneasy, Thomas went back up to his room. The key was still in the lock, and he'd gone out in such a hurry that he'd even forgotten to close the door properly. The shirt and trousers lay on the floor where they had fallen. He was staggered at his own carelessness. What if someone came in and found them? He would never be able to explain why he had cut off the trouser bottoms; and the blood on the collar, how could he explain that? He must get the clothes out of the house and dispose of them. He could stuff them into somebody's dustbin on his way to work—tomorrow morning, ideally, because the dustbins were emptied early on Monday morning. He could do that easily. But the trouser bottoms and the collar, with blood on them, they might attract attention and start inquiries. They would have to be got rid of in some other way. Not merely got rid of—they would have to be destroyed. Accordingly he rolled

---

the shirt and trousers into a bundle and placed it at the foot of the door to make sure he wouldn't forget it the next morning. He hid the other bits and pieces in the cupboard.

Once he had got these things out of the house, of course, the situation would be entirely different and he would be free to consider what was the best course of action. For the time being there was nothing else to be done. Feeling very exhausted, he stretched out on the bed to have a rest, but within seconds he was fast asleep. He slept for twelve hours.

When he awoke his mind was sharp and clear. A shaft of sunlight slanted through the window. Emerging from sleep with his body wonderfully refreshed and his soul untangled, in a state of weightless, motionless transparency reflecting neither memory nor desire, like a pool unencumbered with a surface, he was conscious of the sun and the sharpness of his mind almost as if it were intoxication, and for a few moments he felt happy. The unfamiliarity of this feeling caused him to sit up. It was a piercing feeling. It transfixed him like a sword. But when he sat up it shattered instantly, leaving only a sense of anxious vacancy which nothing he could think of seemed able to fill.

"What can it be? What's missing?"

As he got dressed he racked his brains, trying to locate what it was that was missing. He caught sight of the welfare officer's note on the table.

"Of course! *Came around to see you as arranged, but you were not in.*"

Unthinkingly he picked up the bundle at the foot of the door, closed and locked the door behind him and hurried out of the house. The street was deserted.

What was he going to tell the welfare officer?

At the end of the street he thrust the bundle into a dustbin standing out on the pavement and ran to catch the bus.

Until midday he was kept very busy. It was tedious

---

work, he could do it without thinking, and for just this reason it had a reassuring effect on him. He worked without a pause, mechanically, not thinking of anything. For long stretches at a time it would seem to him that everything was just as it should be; he was doing his work, and there was nothing to worry about. However, as soon as he stopped work to take his lunch break an unsolicited thought, an admission, presented itself to him so perfectly formed that he was unable to resist it.

"This feeling has nothing to do with the welfare officer's note, and it is different from all previous feelings of its kind. It won't be stopped up, now with one thing, now with another, for it has a very particular cause, outside of the feeling itself."

There was no unthinking this thought. Throughout the afternoon it hung there in his mind, luminous and inextinguishable.

Later he was polishing and stacking plates. On one of the plates he noticed a greasy smear. He wiped it with a cloth and held it up to the light. As he did so a thought occurred to him with such force that he let go of the plate and it shattered on the floor.

The police had a record of his fingerprints. When they discovered the body there wasn't the slightest doubt that they would also be able to identify his fingerprints in every room at the top of the house.

"But they haven't discovered the body yet. There may still be time to do something about it."

At three o'clock he finished work and caught the bus. The bus was crowded. Looking out of the window he sat and listened to people talk, and listening to them made him feel safe.

"After all, do something about what?"

And so for the time being he sat tight. Yet however comfortably he tried to arrange this question for himself he was aware all the time of the pointed either-or it attempted to gloss over; hard and becoming harder the further he went, like something gritty in his shoe which he had failed to shake out.

To leave everything as it was, to do nothing about those fingerprints, meant doing a very definite something else: to report the murder immediately, before his traces were found. Then why had he waited almost two days before doing so? Why cut off the collar and the trouser bottoms? And as his landlady had asked, why sneak into the house by the back door? It was an unacceptable consequence.

He got up and sat down again.

"Of course it's better to leave everything just as it is."

Nonetheless, after a short while he stood up again and got off the bus. He walked quickly to the nearest subway station.

Thomas half understood what was happening to him. He knew that it was to his disadvantage; that there was still a chance to change it; and that despite this he would not change it. Something which there had been no reason for beginning now had a reason in the fact that it had begun, and the further he went with it the cloudier the original issue—why had he begun with it then?—became.

He sat in the train and thought to himself: besides, going to the house to remove any traces that might have been left in no way altered the basic facts of the case. For if he had nothing to do with the murder there would not be any traces connecting him with it either. From whatever angle he looked at it the logic of this seemed unchallengeable.

"Whereas if traces *were* left in the house the matter is by no means so clear."

Turning it over and over, as though he had still not decided the matter, he looked up with surprise to find that he was no longer sitting in the train but walking along the road, not more than two or three hundred yards from the house. For some reason the idea of somebody catching him going into the house never occurred to him, perhaps because he had decided that his purpose in visiting the house was merely to make quite sure of the basic facts; at any rate, reassured by the innocence of this purpose, as if it were some kind of talisman that would ward off all harm, he walked straight down the street and through the open gate of the house at the end without meeting anyone.

He went around to the back of the garden and down the basement steps exactly as he had done before. Nothing in the big room had changed. In the corridor he stopped and listened. It was very still. Softly he made his way forward, stopped and listened again. Absolute silence. He ascended the stairs. The hands of the big clock on the landing had stopped at a quarter to six.

Going along the top landing towards her apartment he felt as if he were entering a tomb.

As he passed the threshold of the first room a rather unpleasant odor rose into his nostrils. He had been prepared for the sight, but the peculiar smell was something new.

The body and the severed head lay just as he had left them the day before. Apart from the smell, nothing had changed.

"Only the smell is different," he said with relief.

He took stock of all the objects and surfaces he might unintentionally have touched.

"Although one can't see them the traces are there all right. Whoever was up here and left his mark might just as well have stayed here in person, for all he thinks he can get away with it."

There were no two ways about it. The quicker he got it done and was out of the house the better.

He went into the bathroom and fetched a cloth from under the sink.

He began with the polished surfaces which most easily

marked—glass, mirrors, door handles and the rest. Remembering he had been at the window in her bedroom, he wiped the windows as well, first in the bedroom and then in all the other rooms. That was no problem. But having come this far he began to realize just how many surfaces, with their invisible records, there actually were: the furniture, the light switches and fittings, even perhaps the walls. The wall plaster was smooth; perhaps fingerprints could be traced on it. He didn't know for sure. So he began wiping all the walls.

It was a laborious job and it took a long time. When he got to the last room, where her body lay, it was already half past seven.

Would he be able to get it done before dark? He started on the second wall, with a mounting sense of unease. The tight air in the room made it difficult to breathe, and he was sweating from his efforts. There were two more walls to do and soon the light would begin to fade. His unease became acute. Hurriedly he finished the second wall, and as he turned to start on the third he stumbled over the leg of the corpse.

"Well no wonder—of course!"

He had forgotten about the corpse. Obviously it was the corpse that had been at the back of his mind and made him so uneasy. Gingerly he touched the outstretched arm. There was no denying the corpse. He continued wiping the walls. It made no difference what he was looking at or thinking about, the wall or the corpse or anything else, it was the same unease and always the corpse he was uneasy about.

When at last he had finished wiping the walls he went into the bathroom and replaced the cloth under the sink. The thought crossed his mind that, having come this far, it would be best to dispose of the body, and with the body the uneasy feeling it gave him too.

But even if he were able to dispose of the body there was no getting around the fact that the girl had been murdered. And besides, why should he? He had wiped everything, even the corpse itself and the piece of candle in her hand. There was not a single trace of his having been there. More. *He had not been there.*

Thomas waited in the house for another twenty minutes until it was completely dark. He slipped out of the gate and made his way back to the main road without meeting anybody.

*T*he next few days passed uneventfully. As time slid by he began to doubt whether such a terrible thing could ever have happened. He found no report of the murder in the newspapers. He slept well, went to work as usual, bought himself a new shirt and went to the cinema twice. Even the meeting with the welfare officer, which he had been dreading, turned out to be quite harmless. He sank into a pattern of life that was like an anesthetic, every day an unchanging round of entirely commonplace events.

Throughout August the holiday season continued. Onko had left a week before, and two days later his landlady went away on holiday too. Apart from himself only Mr. Peters and Lisa were left in the house, so he could come and go freely without the unpleasant feeling of being under constant surveillance. For the first time since his arrival at Long Street he felt relaxed.

But on his way home one afternoon he picked up a paper and read that the body of the girl had been found. It did not ruffle him at first. In print the story seemed very remote from his already fading memory of what had happened, and the girl whose picture he saw in the paper was not recognizable as the person he had met that afternoon on the bus. But one thing in the story alarmed him; the word *manhunt,* which cropped up two or three times. Every time he read this word it gave him a peculiar sensation, as if fine strips of skin were being peeled off his forearms.

For several days the story was front-page news. He read about it during his lunch hour. The police appealed to persons who had known the girl or been with her on that evening to come forward. Then the story was moved to an inside page, and after a while there was no mention of it at all. It was only when the reports were discontinued that he again began to feel uneasy.

It was not so much the murder he felt uneasy about as its remoteness from him, his indifference towards it. For days at a time it would be almost entirely absent from his thoughts. Confused by the pictures in the newspapers, which bore so little resemblance to his memory of her, he in turn became doubtful of that memory. Her image began to recede. Finally it was extinguished altogether. He forgot her. And after a fashion he forgot everything else that had happened.

It disappeared from the surface of his mind, he made no attempt to recall it, but it remained with him nonetheless. He was aware of it as an unpresence; instead of the displaced thought itself the slight surface turbulence its displacement had caused, like the tugging of little gusts on the peripheries of a distant storm.

He began to have terrible dreams.

The girl who appeared in these dreams was sometimes dead, sometimes alive, sometimes he killed her himself, sometimes he watched her killed by others. These people were always unknown to him, the circumstances in which they killed her always casual; on a street, at a fairground, wherever, it took place in full view of crowds of people. He watched her being killed many times and in many different ways, and the crowds of people always stood by with the same severe detachment, utterly compassionless. The killing itself was of no account and was soon forgotten. But the feeling of having no feeling, intimations of this appalling void, began to infiltrate and terrorize his daytime.

During these weeks he saw Lisa only once. He came back one afternoon to find her cleaning the hall floor. She spoke to him as he was going past her, and when he brushed her aside and went on upstairs she called after him, but he pretended he had not heard.

That night he dreamed he was in an orchard. The trees bristled with apples, or perhaps they were netted; at any rate, there he was entangled in an apple tree. He knew the place. Nearby stood a summerhouse. The summerhouse had once been open on one side, but where it had been open there was now inexplicably a fourth wall. Other figures moved on the fringe of the dream, indistinctly, as if he could only see them out of the corner of his eye. They filed past the summerhouse and looked in through a window. He had not looked himself, but he knew, without looking, that two people lay dead inside. Still among the apple trees, not moving to look, he nonetheless had a clear image of the interior of the summerhouse. A man was cutting a woman's throat. Somebody came up to him and silently handed him a torch as a sign for him to go and look. He didn't need the torch, he didn't want to look anyway. But after a while he approached the summerhouse window and peered inside. In the soft crepuscular light he could make out their feet and legs; and gradually, as the light rolled back, a torso and a head came into view. Both had been dead for some time. They lay with one arm outstretched and raised, half-burnt matchsticks in their fingers. A sepulchral stillness had settled on them, like a film of dust.

Into this dream intruded the sound of footsteps overhead and a series of sharp reports, the sound of something or someone being struck hard, followed by sobs and cries. It seemed that Lisa was crying and that Mr. Peters was beating her. Unsure if he was awake or asleep, tired even beyond curiosity, he listened to the sounds of him beating her and to the girl's cries and was aware that he must get up to stop it, but already the cries were fading into whimperings and the whimperings into a silence which continued seamlessly into a deeper sleep.

When he woke up the next morning it seemed only a minute ago that he had been dreaming about the summerhouse and imagined he had heard sounds in the room overhead. He jumped out of bed at once and quickly got dressed. As he was making his way downstairs the door of Lisa's room opened and she came out.

"He beat me again!" she whispered fiercely, coming forward and taking hold of his arm.

Thomas stared at her in silence, wishing he were out of the house. Lisa shook him desperately.

"Don't you believe me? Look! Look what he did to me!"

She pulled up the hem of her gown. There were cuts across her buttocks and thighs.

"See?"

"So that was what happened last night," said Thomas slowly.

"You mean you heard it?"

He said nothing.

"But if you heard it you'd've done something. You'd have come up and stopped him, wouldn't you."

Lisa touched his arm and said again, "Wouldn't you?"

He unlocked the front door and left the house without answering her question.

He didn't go to work that day, however. He spent the whole morning on the subway, crossing and recrossing the city. He thought about the dream, how he had heard Lisa being beaten by her stepfather and had lain in bed listening to her cries and had done nothing about it. He thought about the question she had asked him when he left the house. He thought about these things all the time. He could think of nothing else.

After a couple of hours it began to get very stuffy in the

1 5 4

subway. He went up onto the streets and started to walk. He walked for several hours. It was a hot day, and the air in the streets seemed just as close as it had underground. He took off his shirt.

Later he came to the river. He took off all his clothes and sat on a terrace overlooking the river. He had been sitting there naked for quite some time when he was spotted by a policeman, who told him to get dressed again and waited until he had moved on.

In the course of the afternoon he arrived back at the house in Long Street. He went straight up to his room, opened the cupboard and pulled out the collar and trouser bottoms which he had hidden there that Sunday afternoon. According to evidence he gave later he had opened the cupboard with the intention of changing his socks, and had discovered the other things there by accident. He even claimed to have forgotten that he had hidden them in the cupboard, and was shocked and distressed when he realized why they were there.

After making this discovery, which, he said, "settled the matter," he washed, put on a suit and tie and went out to buy a bottle of paraffin.

Then he returned to the house, took the scraps of material he had hidden out into the backyard, poured paraffin over them and set fire to them. This was confirmed by a neighbor, who had watched him from a window.

In burning these scraps of clothing it seemed to have been his intention to destroy, as he explained it, the "decisive evidence" of his connection with a terrible crime. That being the case, it was very remarkable that as soon as he had done so he should have gone straight to the police and confessed to the murder of Nancy Fleming almost three weeks earlier on the night of August the fifteenth:

I murdered the girl.

But whether these were the words he actually used, or

whether the officer on duty heard only three words and understandably interpolated a fourth, could unfortunately not be
established afterwards, on account of an already known anomaly of the young man's speech and the fact that he never volunteered such a confession again.

Havel's first meeting with Onko took place a few days after Thomas N. had been arrested.

Onko had only just got back from his holiday. He was called in by the police to corroborate a number of statements in a lengthy deposition which Thomas had made covering the entire three-and-a-half-month period for which he had any recollection.

Onko's evidence was taken down as a matter of routine. His account of the evening in question tallied with the account given by Thomas, and on the crucial point, namely, that he had not been at the victim's house at all, he was independently confirmed by Pardoe and his girlfriend. They recalled that on the way to Nancy's house they had been asked to drop someone off, and that the man who got off had very nearly been run over as he was crossing the road. Onko enlarged on this incident, explaining that he had failed to see the oncoming car because he was extremely shortsighted. He said he had wanted to get home early as he had an early start the following morning. In short, his statement was satisfactory and did not raise any problems.

Havel was interested in Onko for other reasons. From the deposition that Thomas N. had made it appeared that over a period of more than three months Onko was the only person to be referred to who was not a member of some institution. Thomas even spoke of him as a "friend," although they had met only twice, on the evening of the murder and about a week before. In a document that was otherwise indescribably bleak from start to finish this reference to a "friend," and the uncharacteristic sense of hope that accompanied it, had aroused Havel's curiosity. Possibly the boy had spoken to him about things he had not shared with anyone else.

Onko was surprised to find himself described as Thomas' friend. He said he had originally read about the boy's case in the newspaper. It caught his attention. A couple of months later he had come home one evening and discovered to his astonishment that the boy was now living in the same boardinghouse. Perhaps Thomas had been grateful to him for the genuine interest which he took in his case. They had had a drink together and talked for an hour or two.

"Ah yes," said Havel. "That was on the Sunday evening a week before the murder. Tell me, do you think that Thomas murdered this girl?"

"He says he did."

"But what do you think?"

"I don't know."

"Do you think he could have killed her?"

"Might have? Or do you mean capable?"

"All right, capable."

"Yes."

"Why d'you think that?"

"I think everybody is capable of killing a person."

"And can you think of a reason why he would kill her?"

"No."

"So you think he could have killed her, but in fact he didn't."

"That's not what I said. I think he could have killed her and not had a reason."

"I don't understand. . . ."

"I mean he could have killed her and not had a reason," repeated Onko.

"What does that mean?"

"That he just killed her. That he didn't have a reason."

"Really?" asked Havel with surprise. "D'you really think that's possible? D'you think he could have cut off her head for no reason? Or are you saying that he's a psychopath? Is that why you called him Kaspar?"

"That has nothing to do with it."

Havel leafed through a typescript on his desk.

"Here we are. Kaspar Hauser. That story made quite an impression on him. He even remembered the name. And altogether, he gives a very detailed account of his meeting with you that evening. He seems to have believed that you would be able to help him in some way."

"Detailed account?"

"He was very struck by your appearance, for some reason."

"Appearance? You mean my back?"

"Yes, I suppose that would have been it."

"Well why not say so? My back is not something I'm ashamed of." Onko laughed, apparently passing off this reference to his deformity with good humor, but Havel saw that it had nettled him.

"It's interesting that you should have drawn a parallel to the case of Kaspar Hauser. And there *are* certain parallels. The opium the police found in his case when they first picked him up. The comments on the taste of water. The speech disturbances and so on. But there are also important differences. Certainly, in some respects Kaspar Hauser was not normal, but at least there is an explanation for his peculiar physical and mental condition—it was due to his confinement. At least he could account for it. Whether you believe it or not is another matter. But there is no way of accounting for Thomas N. because he has lost his memory and unfortunately was not carrying a letter that might have helped us. Just conceivably he did share a fate rather like that of Kaspar Hauser, but you have no way of knowing. So why conjecture?"

"Because you have no way of knowing."

"I beg your pardon?"

"Coming to an end of the facts, an end of what you know, you have to jump."

"Jump? Jump where?"

"Into something you don't know. Conjecture."

Havel looked at Onko warily.

"I take it you have a conjecture."

"Of course."

"Then perhaps I might be allowed to benefit from it too."

Onko shrugged.

"As you like. —Suppose, for instance, not that he has lost his memory, but that nothing was ever registered in it as 'past,' and that accordingly there was never anything to lose. Suppose his memory is absolutely intact. Suppose instead that that tract of apparently irrecoverable past, and now, what is present—suppose that both past and present are of such uniform quality, the passage from past into present so smooth and constant that he slides from the one into the other imperceptibly, without ever being aware of the transition or, for that matter, of there being any such transition at all. Suppose that, for instance."

Onko looked intently at Havel, as if expecting all his powers to be fully concentrated on supposing this.

"Suppose that, for whatever reason, Thomas N. had been confined like Kaspar Hauser for the whole term of his natural life; or at least for as much of it as he could be expected to remember. He is confined not in a hovel but, perhaps, on the tenth floor of an apartment block or in the back room of a discreet suburban house. He is well cared for. He has plenty to eat, books, a television perhaps, and a nice view from the window. All he lacks is liberty, company and a telephone. He lacks these, but he doesn't miss them, for that is how it has always been. He sleeps well. And he sleeps a great deal. We might say he vegetates. But then, what else is there for him to do? When he awakes in the morning he always finds the refrigerator full. His keeper comes by night, knowing how soundly his charge sleeps, and replaces what he has eaten during the day. He also pays the rent regularly and makes sure that nothing ever happens to arouse the neighbors' suspicions. He knows his charge will give no trouble because he keeps him sedated. And anyway, why should he? Aware of no other life than the one he is leading there is no reason for him to be dissatisfied.

"But one day it comes to an end. It is decided that the boy must be moved out of the room in which he has been confined. The move is carefully prepared. For weeks or even months in advance the sedation is increased, and he passes the time in a dull twilight, not fully conscious of where he is. And so, after many years of this solitary existence, he is taken sleeping by his keeper one night and left on the streets, where in due course he is found by the police.

"The boy is naturally astonished when he wakes up on the streets. His astonishment soon gives way to a sense of being caught up in a nightmare. For days and weeks he is asked questions, endless questions which he can never hope to answer because they are quite unintelligible. Who are you? Where do you belong? He has no idea what these questions mean, but gradually he learns that almost as important as knowing what they mean is pretending to know what they mean. And perhaps this is right, for after a while they stop asking him these questions and eventually he is given another room.

"In some ways the new room is much like the one he had before, and in some ways it is different. But granting these differences: can he be sure that it is actually a different room? From his point of view, you see, it is more likely he'll think that it's the same room, which in some respects has changed, than

---

a different room which in some respects is the same. The most notable change is the fabulous door through which he can pass in and out, opening onto an unimaginable world, a hitherto nonexistent dimension. What assures you, you see, that he is in your reality? It may be that he inhabits another reality, bound spatially by the limits of a room, beyond which reality ceases to exist exactly as the room itself does, becoming something of an altogether different texture, like a dream, say, on the borders of waking consciousness. It is outside of this room, so to speak, that questions as to his identity and his past are thrust at him, and perhaps that is the only sort of answer he's in a position to give: all this is outside of my room.

"Within this room he may have a quite different conception of time, as a result of his confinement. Perhaps his awareness of time is no more than an awareness of a condition of sameness; the sameness of his room. So his past, as we would call it, is constantly there, in exactly the same sense that the room is there, and is indistinguishable from his present. In fact he dispenses altogether with the notion of time. He lives in a condition of perfect stasis, which for him is nothing other than physical sameness. It must be by means of this idea that he also comes to terms with the changes that are later imposed on him. He does not say: Once it was like this, and now it is like this. He revises his idea, puts it on a broader footing. He says: There are deviations of sameness. It is even conceivable that he thinks of these deviations as being somehow concurrent, which is not altogether illogical, if he is convinced of an underlying sameness. Accordingly all change is of the nature of a superimposition upon that underlying sameness; and since he is only aware of change by being aware *at the same time* that something can have both this aspect and that aspect, he may infer from the fact of these two different aspects being simultaneous in his consciousness that this can only be so if they are actually coexistent.

"And perhaps the evidence supports him."

"The evidence?" inquired Havel ironically. "What evidence?"

"The evidence of quantum theory. Before the development of quantum theory, you see, the only way alternative universes could be envisaged was sequentially. That is the world of Kaspar Hauser. The basis of quantum theory is that a choice is made at random from all the options open to a particle at the quantum level of electrons, photons and so on. The choice may be influenced in certain directions, but any of the options might, in principle, occur. We are now at liberty to contemplate the possibility that whenever such a choice comes up the entire universe splits in two and both choices take place, with two separate universes developing as a result. This is the world of Thomas N. Theoretically it calls for the existence of a multiplicity of parallel but related universes, all originating from a variety of choices at the quantum level, all concurrent, and of course all equally valid. —Suppose *that's* how it stands. What do you say to that?"

But Havel was so astonished at this fantastic presentation of the case that he had nothing to say at all.

*A*fter the police had formally charged Thomas N. with the murder of Nancy Julia Fleming he had appeared before the magistrates' court, where it was decided there was a case against him, and a few weeks later, towards the end of September, he appeared there a second time to be committed for trial. Barring the discovery of new evidence or other unforeseen difficulties, his trial was scheduled to open in the new year. The police investigations therewith came to a close.

The case against Thomas N. was formidable. It was the view of the defense counsel that it would be in their client's interests to approach the case through its complex psychological ramifications. They asked to have access to the records of the clinic where the boy had originally been treated, and thus came into contact with the psychiatrist who had been responsible for him, Dr. Ormond. Subsequently he was retained by the defense as their specialist consultant.

Lack of motive, their client's total inability to explain why he might have murdered the girl, much exercised the defense counsel. Thomas N. offered no explanation of the killing, could tell them nothing about the killing itself, and yet had voluntarily given himself up to the police as the murderer of Nancy Fleming. With curious reluctance he conceded the interpretation which counsel wanted to put on the events: that he had understandably been led to assume he had murdered the girl from the appearances of the case, that although these appearances told strongly against him they were not yet proven, and that accordingly he had no grounds to believe he had done it. Once their client had conceded this he could also be persuaded to retract his original confession and agree to a plea of not guilty.

The question of motive much exercised Havel too. And he had other doubts, which he kept to himself. The official police inquiry was closed, but Havel had not been idle. Several times during those weeks he paid visits to the prison where the accused had been committed for trial.

For twenty minutes they sat facing each other across a table, at first in silence, as the boy refused to answer any of his questions. Havel spent the time looking at the slender hands that lay palms down on the opposite side of the table, the arms, the shoulders, and the eyes, wondering if they had the strength in them and the evil to cut the head off a girl with a few strokes, gouging the floorboard under a thick carpet, and to mutilate the body afterwards with a burning candle.

Gradually the boy had become accustomed to his visitor. Havel no longer asked questions. He waited for the boy to talk.

It was a very peculiar talk. It rambled, without any connection, from one subject to another, showing no awareness of shifting back and forth between identifiable reality and delirious imagination, in stops and starts, often unintelligibly. A bird had died, a child had been born, a man had been locked into a cage and a chair had turned into a severed head. He threw back his head and laughed.

The long warm summer spilled over into September and ebbed very slowly through the first weeks of October. Havel took his holiday at home, sitting out on the roof terrace overlooking the river, surrounded by piles of books. He read them without pleasure, often did not even understand what they were about. In November he could no longer sit outside and continued his reading indoors. He made notes. A pattern began to emerge.

For somewhere in his ramblings the boy had started to talk about *the other lodger* and said something that confirmed Havel in the undertaking on which he had privately set out.

His inquiries began casually with a visit to the premises in Long Street. He asked to be shown over the house. He had not expected to find anything. And he found nothing. But this nothing which Havel found was nonetheless of a kind that interested him. Apart from some clothes in his cupboard, the other lodger had no belongings. Nothing belonged to him. Not a single thing. And he had lived in this room in Long Street for seven years. A quiet lodger, the landlady said.

No belongings. *He could have killed her and not had a reason.*

Havel used the facilities at his disposal to obtain some information about the background of the other lodger.

In the meantime Havel turned his attention to the local branch of the municipal library. It was only ten minutes' walk from Long Street. He filled out a form for a reader's card. And he asked to see the library registers for the past seven years.

He returned to the Flemings' house. For several hours he

sat in the rooms where the girl had been murdered. He walked down from the top of the house to the basement and back up again, several times. And eventually his attention came to rest on a curtained closet on the landing below the top-floor apartment. He drew aside the curtain and rummaged through the objects inside. The closet was used for storing household appliances, unwanted junk and a variety of tools. Forensic experts had already examined the closet, with negative results.

Havel also visited Pardoe and invited himself out for a drive. He asked him to follow the same route he had taken on the evening of August the fifteenth. Pardoe drove him to a semidetached house on the other side of town. Havel stood at the curb and briefly inspected the house. From there they drove in the direction of Nancy's house. On the way he asked to be dropped off at a spot that was specified by Pardoe. He consulted a map and crossed the road.

I failed to see the oncoming car because I'm extremely shortsighted.

Havel looked at his watch and began to walk. He walked at a reasonably brisk pace. And after twenty minutes he again arrived at the Flemings' house. He stood in the garden, looking up at the house. He walked around the house to the stairs leading down to the basement. He began to descend the stairs, but halfway down he changed his mind and walked back around the house to the front door. For a while he remained standing outside the door. This time he did not go into the house. He walked back to the point at which Pardoe had dropped him off, and again consulted his map.

His survey was inconclusive. He knew there would be nothing conclusive. He was looking for a sufficient number, a very large number, of inconclusive pieces. And here he had another. For while it was no great distance, in fact walking distance, as he had just established, from here to the Flemings' house, it would be a long and inconvenient journey for anyone setting off in the opposite direction with the intention of going to Long Street. Not merely that. The journey to Long Street would be very much quicker if one did not come this way at all. It would be very much quicker if one set out directly from that semidetached house.

The facts admitted Havel's interpretation. They allowed a feasibility, at that particular time and on that particular stretch of road. No more than a feasibility.

A choice is made at random.

He arrived at his office one morning to find a file on his desk. It was a very slim file. Havel read it in two minutes. He put the file down and made a telephone call. He spent the morning working at his desk. In the afternoon he caught a train.

Havel sat in the train with a newspaper on his knee. He did not read the columns printed in the newspaper. He read other words, over and over again, which had been printed there by his memory. The subject had arrived in the country as an immigrant, four years old and in the care of friends, shortly after the war. Sole surviving member of his family. Raised by a schoolmaster. Outstanding school record. At the age of seventeen a place at university to study mathematics and philosophy. His foster parent died in the year of his matriculation. Subject left university two years later without graduating. No traceable record of his whereabouts for the next eight years. Presumed to have traveled extensively abroad. Two applications for passport renewal at consulates abroad during this period. Income-tax returns thereafter indicated that the subject had been consistently employed. Two years as hospital porter, subsequently employed as night watchman by a private company. Resident at Long Street throughout this period. Unmarried, not registered as a voter or the owner of a vehicle, no previous convictions.

Havel read the sports page and started a crossword puzzle. One down and three across. The wounds had been inflicted with a quite small instrument such as a chopper or meat cleaver.

Quantum theory and burning candles. Four letters. Havel tossed the newspaper into a corner and got off.

The country house which was the object of his visit accommodated a wrinkled old man and his youthful wife. Would the inspector care for some tea? He would indeed. Havel felt grateful to be diverted into the reassuring normality of tea in a country house after the somber preoccupations of the previous months. His business with the retired professor took less than an hour. And afterwards the professor's wife showed him around the garden.

On his way back in the train Havel read his notes of what the professor had said. He remembered his former student very well. There was a natural disappointment that the most gifted pupil he had ever taught had unaccountably fallen by the wayside, but this disappointment did not sour his judgment.

He had a design, grand and simple: to encompass the entirety of human knowledge.

At the municipal library Havel began to copy entries from the registers. It was a long task. Every evening he sat in the reading room, copying for a couple of hours. The register for the first year alone contained over two hundred entries. Most of the titles were books on logic and the natural sciences. Books on quantum theory and particle physics figured prominently on the list.

From the register for the second year Havel noted as many entries again, a consistent average of four volumes a week. There was a falling off in the number of natural-science titles, an increased interest in mechanics and engineering.

His intellectual habits were predatory. As soon as he had opened one door he hurried on to the next. I had the impression he conceived of knowledge almost as a space to be physically traversed, like some immense building, and so immense that he must have known no man would ever be able to see it in its entirety.

In the course of the fourth and fifth years the annual

total of register entries dropped to a hundred and fifty, and the nature of the titles began to change. The preoccupation with engineering yielded to a stubborn interest in arcane treatises concerned with the perpetuum mobile, the natural sciences were ousted by alchemy, astrology and mystic philosophy. Havel browsed through some of these books. He found them unintelligible.

During the second half of the fifth year the rate of entries escalated rapidly. Between September and April in the following year some two hundred and fifty books had been loaned out. The titles showed a new bias towards ethics and religion and a now obsessive preoccupation with transcendental literature of every kind. The interest of the reader at the municipal library appeared to have gravitated towards matters of a speculative nature beyond the parameters of empirical knowledge; in a word, towards mysteries.

Why should such a man walk around with a knife?

Havel had him followed for a week.

From Monday to Friday the subject's life followed a strict routine. He left Long Street at two o'clock every afternoon and walked to the municipal library, where he spent an hour reading the papers before having his lunch at a cafeteria down the road. Between half past three and five o'clock, on five successive days, he attended matinee performances at a cinema—cartoons, Westerns and sex films. After leaving the cinema he would drop off at a bar for a drink and buy himself sandwiches. He never ate the sandwiches. He put them in his pockets. Between seven and eight he set off for the company where he was employed as a night watchman. Presumably it was during the night hours that he settled down to reading, but during the week in question he was not observed carrying any books. When the cleaners arrived at six o'clock in the morning he left the premises and returned to Long Street.

After lunch on Saturday at his usual cafeteria the subject

had gone to an amusement park. He took rides on the roller coaster and the ghost train, visited the cabinet of horrors and purchased a stick of cotton candy. In the evening he went to a bar in a certain part of town and spent an hour with a prostitute in a room above the premises. On the following Sunday he had not emerged from the house in Long Street at all.

Havel made a visit to the bar and accompanied the same prostitute to a room upstairs. He paid the full time, but was down again in fifteen minutes.

Meanwhile he continued laboriously with his investigations at the municipal library. By the beginning of December he had worked his way to the end of the register for the sixth year and had listed a total of over a thousand books.

He asks me to stroke the hump on his back.

Havel opened the register for the seventh, the current year. January, February. He examined the register with increasing surprise. March. He asked the librarian if there were other registers running concurrently for the same year, but of course there was only this one. His eye slid incredulously down the pages, raced ahead to the end of the register and returned to the beginning. Slowly, unbelievingly, he went through it again. And he went through it a third time. For it was empty, wasn't it? Despite all the names and titles: there was a stupendous hole in it.

He had stopped reading.

In six years he had read over a thousand books. And then he had stopped. For the past twelve months he had not taken out a single book.

After office hours Havel sat alone at his desk with his head in his hands.

Before our ways parted I pointed out to him that even during the two years of our association the building had been enlarged by many more rooms than he had already been into. He would have to make a choice.

Havel took the meager file out of a drawer of his desk

and checked the date of birth. December the twenty-third. His thirty-second birthday. Was that symbolic?

Either that or he would go off his head. Did he, inspector?

Havel replaced the file in his drawer, locked it and turned out the lights.

Sole surviving member of his family.

He left the building and crossed the street. Had there been anything significant about his own thirty-second birthday? Perhaps at around that time the first awareness of a delicate shift of balance, between fading youth and encroaching middle age.

A thousand books. And how many more in the preceding years, of which there was no other record than two applications for the renewal of his passport?

As Havel walked to the station he could not shake off the feeling that he was being followed. He was quite familiar with this feeling. He had had it for several weeks.

Perhaps several thousand books, in all. But not registered as the owner of a vehicle. Unmarried. Employed as a night watchman, thirty-two years closer to his grave.

Dangerously top-heavy. What about the human factor?

He had failed.

Havel paused at the subway entrance, glanced back down the crowded street and stepped onto the escalator.

Too much head. So cut it off.

There was a lack of human interest.

Leaving the problem of what to do with the body. Cotton candy and prostitutes, cabinet of horrors. A burning candle and a heap of dolls. The magnitude of such a failure might explain the ferocity of such a revenge. Not blind revenge, exactly; but extremely shortsighted.

The doors of the subway closed. Havel began to walk back down the train in the direction he had come from.

Mature too early and childish too late. A gross mind in

a gross body. He had made his choice, but it had not been at random. Havel knew that now, having become the cosmographer of his mind. Over a long period of gestation the night watchman had arrived, by a process which reason could follow, at a singularity in the icy interstellar spaces, a black hole of sorts, which lay beyond reason but was at the same time inescapable.

Havel reached the last car. It was empty. He glanced at his watch. Of course: it was already half past seven. He took a newspaper out of his coat pocket and completed the crossword puzzle he had begun earlier that day.

A few stops down the line he got off and surfaced to the chilly night air. He could smell the river. At the corner of his apartment block he involuntarily turned and looked down the empty road.

Had he been imagining things? Had it all happened in his imagination?

He took a pair of binoculars from the shelf and went out onto the terrace. He focused the binoculars on the wharves half a mile down on the other side of the river. Strange, this proximity. Elective affinities. His night watchman would acknowledge the principle if not the man. Through the murky night Havel made out the warehouse where a light always burned in a window on the second floor.

Already the weekend. The trial of Thomas N. opened on Monday. In view of the evidence the boy would probably be convicted. Havel saw the case for a conviction very clearly himself.

Despite all, just a feasibility, despite all. The results of his private investigation were useless unless he outsmarted his man.

He put his feet up on the table and smoked a cigar.

But there was one point where he could broach him: his intellectual hubris.

Havel phrased a letter in his head: at their last meeting / the night watchman had indicated a view of crime / which in his professional capacity greatly interested him. / Perhaps he would care to come and discuss this topic in more detail over dinner. / Yours et cetera.

He posted the letter to Long Street that night. And a few days later, as he expected, Onko accepted the invitation.

But after all, Thomas N. took his seat at nine o'clock on Monday morning knowing no better than anyone else in court if he had committed the crime for which he was being put on trial.

From the public gallery came a rustling and humming, the sound of a great swarm as it sorted and settled itself, checkers of light and shadow that gradually assembled into a smooth honeycomb of white faces. Here and there he could just squeeze in with his eyes and recognize two or three of the visitors with a shock of familiarity, the assistant master, the police inspector, the man with the split face—and all of them quite a distance, it seemed, a very great distance away. But where was Onko? And perhaps Nancy would have been there if she were not dead. Thomas laughed. He scribbled a note and passed it over to his counsel. For of course the death of Nancy was the subject of his trial.

But it was not a laughing matter at all. In the course of the morning he began to wonder if there had been a mistake and they had brought him into the wrong courtroom.

For the decision as to whether he was innocent or guilty very quickly ceased to have anything to do with him. His trial took its course with an assurance he knew the matters it dealt with entirely lacked. A trial had to have an outcome. This foreknowledge of the absolute certainty of there being an outcome, a certainty existing nowhere outside the abstract framework of law, impressed Thomas as being a great deal more important than the nature of the outcome itself.

He was immediately put at a disadvantage. The certainty of the law was personified by the public prosecutor, and thus inevitably took the form of a certainty of guilt. The accused was guilty at first for procedural reasons; the prosecution must be allowed to assume what it would later be required to prove. In this undertaking the prosecution would take full advantage of what was apparently a neutral fact but in practice a powerful bias against the accused, regardless of the merits of his case: the fact that a crime had taken place at all. The process of law being concerned with the reconstruction of events which had undoubtedly taken place, the formal position of the prosecution that somebody had done something and had a reason for doing it would always be inherently more plausible than the position of the defense that somebody had *not* done something, whatever reasons he may or may not have had. —What reasons could he have for not doing it, if it had been done? —And in addition to this, as Thomas instinctively grasped when he got up to reply to the charge, the accused was already compromised merely by virtue of being charged with the crime and having to deny it; he was forced into association with the crime by the act of denying the crime.

Thomas did not like the look of the public prosecutor at all; and the strange clothes he was wearing were distinctly ominous. Surely the words he was saying would have had a quite different effect if he had not been wearing those clothes. And of course it was not true that the prosecution was wearing the same clothes as the defense, it was the other way around, the defense was wearing the same clothes as the prosecution.

The prosecution proposed dividing the evidence into four phases: the general background to the case, the events immediately leading up to the murder, the murder itself and the behavior of the accused after the crime. The crime he was here alleged to have committed would therefore be represented above all as a *consequence*. Accordingly it would be necessary for the court to examine the fourteen-week period from the appearance of the accused in June to his (since retracted) confession in September in its entirety. As nothing was known about him prior to this period the court would effectively be concerned with his life in its entirety, and in this sense, therefore, *he was on trial for his life.*

Rustling and humming in the gallery. Thomas looked up with a shock. The public prosecutor took off his spectacles. Everything about the accused, he said, turning to address him personally, even the most trivial examples of his behavior, as the prosecution would now proceed to show, was relevant to an understanding of his crime.

He waited until the court was silent, put on his spectacles and resumed.

The background to the case: this would cover the period between the day the accused was first picked up by the police and the day of his departure from the home for maladjusted children where he had been temporarily accommodated. The court would hear the evidence of the police officer who first questioned him and who discovered opium in his possession. A lot of attention must be paid to the subject of drugs and drug abuse, as they played a central part in the case. Further, to the evidence of the doctor who originally examined the accused and volunteered the opinion that he had possibly been "exposed to drugs over quite a long period," and that he could in consequence be expected to have led "a very irregular life." It was on the strength of this opinion that he was admitted to a psychiatric clinic for observation. The prosecution would in due course be questioning specialists and members of staff in connection with certain incidents that had occurred there. For example, had there been any indications that the accused was prone to violent behavior? That he was in any way sexually disturbed? That he was congenitally deceitful? That he was unsociable and secretive? The court would learn that all these questions could be answered in the affirmative, and that among the various reasons for the decision to discharge him from the clinic professionally qualified persons had expressly drawn attention to "his intractable manner and refusal to cooperate." The court would hear the same opinion expressed by a large number of people, among them the experienced welfare officer who had taken over responsibility for the accused after his discharge and found him employment and accommodation.

They would also have occasion to consider why it was that the accused had been content to accept a very menial position instead of applying for some vocational training or making an effort to learn something more rewarding. Granted, he was known to be suffering from amnesia, and to that extent one could justly speak of an impairment of his mental capacity. On the other hand, it must be pointed out that none of those who had examined him or had closer dealings with him had ever suggested that as a result of this defect his intelligence and natural ability to learn were negatively affected. At both the clinic and the special school, however, he had not only shown no interest in but deliberately flouted all attempts to help him.

The burden of the evidence which the court would hear in connection with some of these episodes was of a moral kind; it concerned the character of the accused. The prosecution wished to remind the jury that although such moral judgments did not have any direct bearing on the issue of whether the accused had actually committed the crime he had been charged with, they ought nonetheless to be borne in mind when considering a second question, whether the accused was *capable* of such a crime. In view of the inconclusive nature of the evidence concerning the crime itself, the answer to this question would necessarily carry considerable weight.

———

Having elaborated the background to the case, the prosecution suggested the court turn its attention to the chain of events that began on the afternoon of August the fifteenth and ended with the murder of Nancy Fleming on the night of the fifteenth to the sixteenth.

The meeting between the accused and the murdered girl seemed to have been pure chance. They had got into conversation on a bus and stayed together for the rest of the day. The accused claimed that the girl was in a peculiar state of mind, which he later had reason to believe was due to her having taken drugs. They went to the house of a man whose main interest in the girl seemed to have been as a client whom he supplied with drugs. Drugs were used on this occasion too. Later it was suggested they go to a party.

On his own admission the accused had not really wanted to go to this party, and he felt no obligation towards the girl either. So why did he go? The question was worth considering, because his indecisiveness at this moment was to have fatal consequences. The prosecution was in no doubt as to the answer: the accused was already in that state of apathy characteristic of the effect of opiates, and was no longer in full control of himself or his actions. These effects were afterwards compounded by alcohol and other dangerous stimulants in such a way as to make his behavior entirely unpredictable.

He had no sooner arrived at this party than he decided to leave, having suddenly remembered that he had arranged to meet a friend in a bar that evening. The girl went with him. Witnesses who were in the bar at the time described the girl as being on the verge of collapse. If the accused had been genuinely concerned for her well-being one might have expected him to try to reason with her or to intervene in some way. But he was not in a much better state himself, and he made no attempt to help her. When she suggested that they return to the party, and when she later invited a group of people to her own house, the accused was swept along like everybody else by a tide of events he was powerless to escape.

Who were these people whom the girl had invited to her house? They were complete strangers, but at the same time she had a lot of things in common with them. They were young, they shared the same habit of drugs, the majority of them lacked any regular occupation, led very self-indulgent lives, despised any idea of restraint or moderation, and were without any sense of commitment to anything other than the pursuit of their own pleasure and the belief that they were exempt from the demands of a society it was their privilege to exploit. Some of them were known to have criminal records, and on the evening in question nearly all of them had broken the law. Their private lives were of no concern to the prosecution, but it was important to draw attention to the kind of company the accused had been keeping that night in order to put the enormity of the crime into perspective. The circumstances in no way excused the crime, but they offered at least a partial explanation. Without the party, without the drugs, without that giddy vortex of recklessness and total abandon which the accused had allowed himself to be sucked into it was doubtful whether such a terrible deed could ever have been committed.

Nancy Fleming had last been seen alive at a quarter to two on Sunday morning. She was seen making her way upstairs, in company with the accused, to her own apartment at the top of the house. After that she had not been seen, either dead or alive, by any of the guests other than the accused, so the vital question of when and how she had met her death could only be answered by one witness—the evidence of the accused himself.

According to his sworn statement the accused had woken up early on Sunday morning and found Nancy Fleming dead. He remembered nothing of what had happened the previous night. The prosecution had no intention of challenging his statement at present, but in the course of the trial the jury would have to decide whether or not they believed it. Assuming his statement to be true, it still left completely open the crucial question of whether he himself believed he had killed her, and for this reason the behavior of the accused after the crime took on a particular significance.

Had he later acted like a person who was confident he was not guilty of any crime? Or did his behavior give one reason to suspect that he was by no means so sure of his innocence? And if not sure, why not?

What had he done when he woke up and discovered the body? He had taken a bath. Why? Because he was covered in blood. What had he done next? He had cut pieces of material out of his shirt and trousers. Why? Because they were stained with blood. He had then attempted to clean up the apartment; he had made the bed and scrubbed out the bath. Why did he do these things? Why did he decide to go to the police and then, when it came to it, not have the courage to report the murder? On returning to his lodgings he had slipped in by the back door —on his own admission it was the first time he had used this door. What possible reason could there be to do this, if not to avoid being seen entering the house? And why should he want to avoid being seen?

The following day he had returned to the house and systematically wiped all the fingerprints. The cover-up was done with such thoroughness that one could not resist the impression he wanted to obliterate the traces of the crime from his own mind. For a short time he might even have succeeded, but the body was eventually found and of course there were reports of the murder in all the national newspapers. He read the reports himself, cold-bloodedly ignored repeated appeals for persons having any information to pass it on to the police. In view of this one could hardly be expected to believe that it had ever at any time seriously been his intention to come forward with that information voluntarily. And even his last act, his confession, which he first made and then later unmade, had to be treated with misgiving. For even if he had not given himself up it would still have been only a matter of hours before the police arrived to question him. His confession was scarcely a voluntary act. It had been forced on him by the hopelessness of his situation.

Why had he behaved like this? Was it the behavior of a person who remembered *absolutely nothing* about the actual occurrence of the crime? Wasn't it far more probably the behavior of someone who did in fact remember something of how that crime had happened? Something? Enough to cut the collar out of a shirt? Quite a lot more than something? Enough to be able to stomach another sight of the mutilated corpse and return to the house to cover his traces? Why these half measures? Why not suppose that the accused was lying in his teeth and remembered perfectly well what had happened that night?

Scattering these questions between little pauses, confident they would all settle with exactly the effect exactly where he intended, the counsel for the prosecution thoughtfully smoothed his gown and sat down, and the court was adjourned.

On the third morning of the trial the defense called its chief witness, the psychiatrist Dr. Ormond. The exchanges between counsel and the witness sometimes fell so thick and fast that Thomas had the greatest difficulty in following.

Was the witness familiar with the exact wording of the defendant's original, since retracted, confession?

He was.

Then would he kindly repeat it.

I murdered the girl.

Did he, the witness, have any reason to doubt that the defendant could have made such a statement?

He did.

Did his doubts attach to the statement itself or to the nature of its wording?

To the wording.

How did the witness think the defendant's statement had more probably been worded?

Murdered the girl.

Would he repeat that, please.

Murdered the girl.

Had the witness, in the course of his psychiatric examination of the defendant, carried out an analysis of his speech behavior?

Yes.

What was the most striking conclusion of that analysis?

He never used the first personal pronoun.

Had this speech anomaly frequently given rise to cases of ambiguity?

Yes.

What sort of ambiguity?

It was unclear who was the agent of the action described.

"It was unclear who was the agent of the action described," repeated counsel, looking around the court.

"And did this apply, without exception, to all the defendant's statements?"

"Yes."

"So it would apply equally to a confession of murder?"

"Yes."

"Thank you. No further questions at this point."

In the afternoon counsel resumed his examination of the witness. Dr. Ormond described to the court the defendant's physical and mental condition at the time of his committal to the clinic. He was picked up off the streets, destitute and suffering from amnesia. The defendant had been in a highly disturbed state of mind, which at first they had been inclined to regard as concomitant with the amnesia. All reported cases of global amnesia documented the patient's confusion about his own identity to a greater or lesser degree. Even in extreme cases, however, the patient remained able to state at least that much about himself: I do not know who I am. The inability of Thomas N. to refer to himself forced them to consider another hypothesis.

"And what hypothesis was that?" inquired the defense counsel.

"That a symptom as consistent as this, and with such precise demarcations, could not be accounted for by any inherent defect of the memory as such."

"Which is to say?"

"We did not think he had forgotten the use of the word 'I,' *but that he had never acquired it.*"

An audible murmuring rose from the crowds in the public gallery. The court was called to order.

"What other considerations might support such a hypothesis?" continued the defense.

"We must assume that his previous history has been a very extraordinary one. We would not say that the defendant is abnormal, but rather that he has been abnormally conditioned. Our impression is of a person familiar with modern civilized life who is at the same time a complete stranger to even the minimal requirements of human society. His condition forces us to assume that he has hitherto lived in utter isolation, which is only imaginable in a state of confinement."

At this point the judge intervened with an instruction to counsel to desist from this line of questioning as it was not material to the issues facing the court.

"Then let us hear from Dr. Ormond about the emotional

state of a person suffering from amnesia. What feelings does such a patient characteristically have?"

"Feelings of bewilderment, coupled with unease."

"And in the case of the defendant?"

"Acute unease. His existence takes on a nightmare quality; he is severed from his past; his own self is inaccessible to him. Under these circumstances it is unsurprising that he is possessed with a persistent fear, exacerbated in the defendant's case by a predisposition to feelings of guilt."

"Guilt? Guilt about what?"

The witness hesitated.

"It is not guilt as we ordinarily understand it, for it has neither cause nor object outside itself. To avoid confusion I refer to it instead as *self-inquisition*. Like normal consciousness, it has a mediating function, supplying itself as the object of its own contemplation. But unlike normal consciousness, the relationship it effects between self and self is characterized not by mutual acceptance but by mutual antipathy."

"In other words, such a person doesn't like himself very much."

"One could put it like that."

"Is this how you would describe the defendant's consciousness of himself?"

"Yes."

"This is his sense of his own identity?"

"Identity—if I might enlarge on this point—"

"Please."

"Identity is not a thing, but a process. It means the quality of being the same. Accordingly it involves two elements, and a reciprocal interaction between those elements. One might describe identity as self-knowledge, albeit without the usual ethical connotations. But when self-knowledge takes the form of self-inquisition, a person's sense of identity extends as far as and no farther than his sense of guilt. The plaintiff represents an extreme example of this case."

"His sense of identity extends as far as and no farther than his sense of guilt," repeated counsel slowly. "Then are you suggesting he *needs* this sense of guilt?"

"It is of existential importance. It is his mind's water and light."

"Guilt as a kind of photosynthesis, as a condition of life?"

"That is an appropriate analogy."

"How can he need a guilt if, as you tell us, it is not *about* anything?"

"Initially it is not about anything. It is the form of perception through which he experiences the world. But since how we perceive always conditions what we experience, a perception characterized by guilt will supply an experience of the world that is likewise of a guilty nature. This is a tautology, just as the process it describes is circular: the subject feels guilty about his own existence."

"His own existence?"

"And whatever substantiates it."

"For example—his memory?"

"For example his memory."

"And what does he do about it?"

"He loses it."

"For example his own shadow on the ground?"

"For example that."

"What does he do about that?"

"He stays indoors."

"For example a severed head on a chair? A collar with blood on it? What does he do when he wakes up one morning and finds a corpse in the house?"

"He covers his traces."

"Why does he do that?"

"Because he does not want to be found out."

"Because he does not want to be found out."

Counsel paused for a few seconds, and added casually:

"Knowing, of course, that he is guilty of the crime. Am I right?"

"On the contrary. Precisely because he is innocent of it."

An uproar immediately broke out in the public gallery, not subsiding for several minutes. The judge threatened to have the court cleared if there were any further disturbances, and instructed the defense counsel to continue with his examination of the witness.

"Dr. Ormond, I asked you why you believed the defendant had covered his traces in the house when he discovered the corpse of a murdered girl. Your answer may have given rise to a misunderstanding. Perhaps we should clarify this point. . . ."

"Certainly. I began by stating my opinion, which I had already formed in my capacity as the psychiatrist responsible for Thomas N. during his stay at the clinic, that he felt guilty about his own existence. The court has heard the evidence I submitted in support of this opinion; it shows to what lengths the defendant went to pass unobserved, to keep—however remote from common sense this may sound—his own existence a secret. Accordingly he was in the habit of covering his traces. This was what I meant when I said that he did not want to be found out. —But of course it is a hopeless undertaking, and from any point of view other than the defendant's own a quite meaningless one. His existence is not a secret, and certainly not a guilty one. Objectively there were never any reasons why he should need to cover his traces. But such is the nature of his obsession. And it happens to coincide with a situation in which there are apparently very powerful reasons why he *should* cover his traces—the murder of a girl under circumstances that suggest he might himself have killed her. Expert in the self-persuasion of guilt, he appropriates the murder for his own purposes. How, knowing all that we do know about the defendant, can we expect him *not* to have assumed that he had done it? Here is a stupendous crime, a very specific, a horrifically palpable act, a crucible, as it were, in which hitherto insubstantial feelings of guilt are hypostatized and fired to such a heat that they adhere irremovably to the sides of the vessel—to a corpse—to a butchery—to a dreadful admission. For at last he *knows*. There is an end of suspicions, doubts, misgivings, an end of self-inquisition, poleaxed by certainty and brute fact. He can no longer escape responsibility for his own existence."

The witness paused.

"This, in my opinion, is the nature of the confession which Thomas N. volunteered to the police three weeks after the murder of Nancy Fleming."

Throughout the hearing of this evidence the defendant sat transfixed, staring at the courtroom ceiling.

At the end of the first week of the trial Havel paid Thomas N. a final visit in prison. He attempted to cheer him up. His prospects were definitely looking up, he thought. The evidence of Dr. Ormond had succeeded in making a breach in the case of the prosecution, and there might yet be the chance of an acquittal. But the boy was dispirited. Perhaps he had not understood the thrust of counsel's examination of the witness at all.

Havel gently steered his attention back to Long Street. The boy talked incoherently about a girl called Lisa and the invalid stepfather who beat her in a room upstairs. But Havel was not interested in what had gone on upstairs. He wanted to know what had happened on the landing outside the boy's room.

"Tell me again exactly what happened that night."

Later he made his way back home. Deep in thought, he traveled a long way past his station and had to catch the train back.

The landing is the weak spot, thought Havel, on the landing, that evening, he was momentarily caught off guard, and in that moment he had betrayed something that surely cannot have been anything other than—Fear.

He put on an apron and began cooking.

I shall make a stew, he decided. He started to peel onions.

If he were afraid, then of course he might want to walk around with a knife.

Somehow it was unsatisfactory, the peeled onions slithered out of his grasp. Havel sliced them and turned his full attention to the green peppers.

What memories might a four-year-old child have brought with him, his cap in one hand, his fate in the other, entrusted to the person who had led him? What memories in the childish head of the sole surviving member of his family, which had escaped the attention of the customs officer? Not childish memories, for sure, not childish at all, which he had unhappily smuggled through customs into his adult life. Frogs and snails and puppy dogs' tails and an unwholesome preoccupation with death, that was what such memories might be made of.

He chopped the gristle off a slab of beef and sliced it into cubes. Undeniably, here he had the base for a very strong stew.

The stew simmered in the pot throughout the afternoon.

He read reports of the trial in the newspapers. The arguments developed by the defense did not read as convincingly in print as they had sounded in court. Imperceptibly subtlety began to slide into sophistry. The nature of the argument made it difficult to summarize. The nature of the case made it difficult to judge. The omens did not look good for the accused.

At four o'clock he took the pot off the stove and sampled a teaspoonful of the stew. Perhaps it could do with a sprinkle of salt.

Perhaps a great many other things too. He changed his mind and sprinkled the salt back into the box. This was a matter of individual taste.

He would leave his guest to salt the stew for himself.

He lay down on the sofa and put everything out of his mind. He had laid the table and cooked the stew, there was nothing left to do. Eventually he fell asleep.

Onko arrived a few minutes after seven. He remained standing on the doorstep as if he was unsure whether he wanted to come in. He had on a tall felt hat, curiously old-fashioned, and was wearing an attempt at a tie.

"Have a drink," suggested Havel.

He showed his guest around the apartment, the odds and ends of his life that had gathered there on its shelves. Onko gave no sign of interest. Havel led him out onto the terrace instead. It was a cold, brilliantly starlit night.

"I expect you know your way around here."

"I work just across the river."

He pointed to the warehouse half a mile away where a light was burning on the second floor.

"An old man comes in over the weekends. He's there now."

"Isn't it really a job for old men?"

"For old men and astronomers. That's why I'm a night watchman. I like to watch the stars. I keep a telescope in the elevator housing on top of the roof."

His glasses flashed as he turned from the dark towards the light.

They went back inside.

Onko sat on the edge of his chair with his fingers just touching the surface of the table. Havel saw the cloth of his jacket stretch across the bulge between his shoulders.

"May I inquire how you acquired your . . . ?"

"I did not acquire it. I played an entirely passive part."

"Oh."

"It was acquired for me. I was dropped out of a train window when I was a baby."

"How very unfortunate."

"On the contrary. At the cost of this minor disfigurement I was thus given a chance of survival."

"Where was the train going?"

———

Onko made an impatient gesture with his hand.

"That is a detail, that belongs to the merely phenomeno-logical order of things."

"What an extraordinary thing to say!" protested Havel, genuinely amazed. "And what a wrong thing to say."

Onko glanced at his watch.

"Shall we begin dinner?" he asked abruptly.

"Whenever you like."

Havel went into the kitchen and made an effort to control his temper. Onko had been in the house only ten minutes and had already succeeded in provoking him. That was the last thing he wanted. He looked through the kitchen door and saw his guest hunched over the table, reading the newspapers. He still had his hat on.

Let the man in the hat talk.

"Have you seen the reports of the trial?" he called through the door.

"I am just looking through them now."

Havel came out with two plates.

"I noticed you were in court yesterday. What was your impression of the witness?"

"Apparently he sought to establish a relationship between identity and aggression."

"Between consciousness and guilt, I thought."

"It goes deeper than that."

Havel sat down.

"Consider," said the man in the hat, his spoon poised, "the objects in this room, ourselves included. They are all iden-tifiable by their mass, by the air which they displace. Where they cease to do so they cease to exist. The intrusion of an object on its surroundings makes possible its existence. The borders that encompass what it is exclude whatever it is not. It belongs to itself only because other does not belong to it. Exis-tence is fundamentally of the nature of aggression. In human terms, whenever a conscious identity begins to doubt its contours it will seek to clarify them through acts of aggression."

He scalped the slice of melon and disposed of it in three or four mouthfuls.

"And that might seem to point a way through the wreckage of *breathtaking crimes* which litter our recent history. Perhaps it does, for part of the way. But after a while we peer down from our rational structures, our explanations of cause and effect, and see ourselves suspended precariously on a catwalk traversing the terrifying moral void which has opened up beneath us. In these, as I should like to call them, *exemplary* crimes, in the sense that they have set a standard which we can never expect to surpass, it is otiose to look for a motive. At most perhaps we can discern a motive force. It is the force of pure unreason, wayward, arbitrary, destructive—and so the stage is set for the appearance of the Modern Crime. To discuss which you invited me to dinner."

"If you are ready, we might go on to the stew," murmured Havel. He carried their plates into the kitchen and emerged with a tureen.

"What is the Modern Crime?" he asked, placing the tureen on the table.

"The Modern Crime is the crime with no motive."

"I consider that an impossibility."

"I know. I will tell you my views," said the man in the hat, taking the ladle his host passed him, "and then you will tell me yours. Agreed?"

"Agreed."

Onko helped himself to the stew.

"But of course! How absentminded of me!"

Havel got up again and fetched a box of matches from the dresser.

"I forgot to light the candles."

He faced his guest across the table, struck a match, and

leaning forward to light the candles noticed the blurred reflection of the flame flare and scatter through Onko's lenses.

"More festive—don't you agree?"

Havel picked up his spoon.

"Then let us begin."

"The crime with no motive," said Onko slowly, "is best illustrated by a case history. Interesting samples can be found in the literature, for example the Bjorkland case, but usually they are flawed: by pathological quirks in the individuals concerned."

"Crimes that have no apparent motive are not usually, but always, flawed by such quirks, I would think . . ."

"Ah, but exactly."

Onko stirred his stew.

" 'Apparent' is your qualification. I am talking about crimes that have *no motive*."

"How can you be so sure about that?"

"By considering a crime that was carried out as an experiment, under scientific conditions, to establish just that point."

"Then that was its motive."

"That might have been its motive. But it depends, doesn't it, on the skill of the experimenter and the rigorousness of his methods. I knew the man in question. I can vouch for his disinterestedness. And I can vouch for his sanity. He was as normal as the next man. He had no criminal inclinations, and until the year when he began to prepare for his experiment he took not the slightest interest in crime.

"This man was a philosopher. His preoccupation with crime began one day when he asked himself the question: what is the most arbitrary, the least necessary thing that a human being can do? This question seems to have arisen when he was considering the possible ethical implications of recent developments in particle physics. Human beings being what they are, his question naturally had to be qualified in terms of individual temperament. He qualified it in terms of himself. The most arbitrary thing, he decided, must be the thing he least wanted to do, the thing most contrary to his fundamental instincts. And the fundamental instinct was that of survival, of life. In this way he arrived at the answer: an action that terminated life."

"Will you have some more?"

"Thank you."

He has appetite, exulted Havel, he is going to take the bait whole.

Onko looked up quizzically.

"But whose life?"

"Whose life?"

"Whose life was to be terminated? In the nature of things one might expect it to be his own. But not in his nature. He was a very phlegmatic man. He was content with his life, as far as it went, and he knew that that was not at all far. He had a clear sense of its perspective; that is to say, of its utter insignificance. He had no wish to die, but he was not afraid of death. And for that matter he didn't have any particular *wish* to live either. In this respect he was a good philosopher, balanced equivocally between now and—and after. The answer to his question was accordingly not suicide but murder.

"Suicide was thinkable and doable. Murder was thinkable. But was it doable? The only way he could establish this would be to commit a murder himself.

"The idea of the wholly arbitrary, wholly unnecessary act had originally had nothing to do with murder. Now that he came to consider it, however, he realized that murder was *the* act in need of a compelling reason. Thus, if it could be done entirely without motive, it must be the act of least necessity and greatest unreason. As the act of a psychopath, however, performed impulsively and with indifference, it was inadmissible. It must be carried out by a normal man fully aware that it was a terrible thing he was going to have to do.

———

"And here he found himself in a dilemma. For wasn't the mere thinking of such an idea as the entirely unmotivated murder already a sign of psychopathic mentality? The question 'Is the motiveless murder doable?' was itself tendentious. The motive could be argued, as you have said, to lie in the proof. And he had other misgivings. Might he perhaps be committing murder for the excitement of it? For an almost erotic sensation of fear? Having fixed the murderous deed in his sights, you see, he had begun to experience agonizing premonitions, at the mere thought of what he was going to do; and very peculiar sensations, as if an octopus were sucking in the walls of his stomach; which at the same time he described as not wholly disagreeable. The balance between arbitrariness of the act and resistance to the act was disturbed, the unreason of the act came to be eclipsed by fear of the act. And so it remained for a long time.

"These uncertainties held him up for about half a year. He had to suspend all his other work. And then the fear gradually began to pass, emotionally he had already gone through with the deed. He had swallowed the octopus whole and discharged it from his system. Even, he was confident, the feelings that would come after: he had *anticipated* remorse. A very extraordinary feat! At last he felt free to act. He would walk out one day with the intention of posting a letter or buying a loaf of bread and would kill someone instead."

Havel watched Onko impassively drink off a glass of wine.

It seemed to have become very warm in the room. Havel got up and opened a window.

"There is one thing," he said, "which your experimenter has not yet taken into account: the views of his victim."

"But they are self-evident. Of course the victim would not approve of the experiment. But he did not see this as relevant to the issue."

"Remarkable. . . . And was the experiment carried out?"

"At the second attempt."

"At the *second* attempt!" exclaimed Havel. "Were you informed about all this?"

"Not about the second, successful attempt. That would have gone beyond my role as an impartial observer. I would thereby have become an accessory, wouldn't I."

"No less in the case of an attempted murder."

"No."

Onko poured himself another glass of wine.

"For nothing happened that could be construed as an attempted murder. It remained a merely putative act in the mind of the experimenter."

"But murder had nonetheless been the experimenter's *intention.*"

"Yes."

Onko paused.

"I will tell you about it, if you are interested."

"I would be very interested."

Havel rummaged in a box and pulled out a cigar, fiddled nervously with the wrapping, keeping his hands moving so that the man in the hat would not notice how they had begun to tremble.

"The victim was selected by a throw of dice."

"I beg your pardon?"

"Three throws, in fact. And these three throws gave an aggregate number—eleven, I seem to remember. The experimenter set off for the town center and waited at a certain arch. The eleventh person to pass through this arch would be his victim. We can take it that he adopted a similar procedure on both occasions. Of course he could have chosen a victim without this rigmarole. But it seemed to him that a quite motiveless act required a quite arbitrary method of execution.

"The eleventh person to pass through the arch turned out to be a middle-aged man carrying a brown paper parcel. It was a question of following this man until he offered the experimenter an opportunity to kill him.

"He had to wait a long time for this opportunity. Several hours."

Onko got up and began to walk about the room.

"For the man met a friend outside a cinema and went to see a film. The friend called out 'Paul!' to attract his attention, so the experimenter now learned his victim's name. This was totally . . . unexpected. He realized it was less easy to kill someone when you knew his name. It put him off his stroke. And perhaps it accounts for the curious fact that afterwards he was unable to remember a single thing about the film he had seen—sitting a couple of rows behind the victim, and the victim's friend.

"When the film was over he followed them to a restaurant. It turned out that the brown paper parcel was a present for the friend. And these details—the victim's name, the parcel and so on—had the effects of personalizing the issue in a way that the experimenter found extremely . . . extremely disturbing. When the two men eventually left the restaurant and he got up to follow them something quite unaccountable happened. For several seconds he was unable to move.

"Outside the restaurant the two men parted and set off in opposite directions. It was a few minutes past ten o'clock. He followed the man down into the subway and caught the same train going out in the direction of the suburbs. He sat in the same car as the man, but at the opposite end. In the middle of the car were two old women, talking in a language he didn't understand. He listened to the women talking and read the advertisements in the car and thought about how he would kill the man sitting at the other end. It was a wet evening—chilly for the time of year—which was just as well—because the knife he was carrying would have been less easy to conceal if he had not been wearing a coat. He could have killed the man right there, but for the women talking on and on in their foreign language. —Perhaps there would be an opportunity on the platform; or in the tunnel leading to the escalator. But when at last the man got off the two women got off as well.

"So he followed the man at a distance of about fifty yards, out into the street—and almost lost him at the first corner. They walked along a main road for a few minutes before turning off left, right and left—into a maze of narrow streets where it suddenly became much quieter and somehow also darker. He was aware of a new smell. The maze of little streets seemed to be surrounded by a park. It was the smell of wet leaves. The rain had left off, but the trees were still dripping.

"He had gradually been catching up, and he was not more than about twenty yards behind the man when he disappeared through an archway leading into a courtyard. For a few seconds he waited in the shadow of the archway from where he watched the man cross the courtyard and enter the building on the opposite side. He was expecting him to have to unlock the door, but it seemed to be already open. As soon as the man had gone through the door he ran across the courtyard and slipped in after him."

Onko paused.

"His description of what follows was particularly vivid— the moment he entered the house he felt an almost electric sensation, a surge of power, as if a dynamo had been switched on inside him, pumping the blood from his chest to the tips of his fingers and the roots of his hair. It seemed to be boiling under his scalp. He could see the man at the turning of the stairs. He unbuttoned his coat. He took out the knife and held the blade up his sleeve. Before he was aware of it he was already halfway up the stairs, as if he had been caught up and hurled forward by the motion of a tremendous wave. As he turned up the second flight his eyes came level with the floor of the landing above and he saw that the borders of the linoleum were cracked and had been filled with some kind of paste, and beyond was the man, reaching into his pocket, his back to the stairs and his coat pushed up on the side where he was reaching into his pocket, showing a brilliant crimson lining facing out. His eyes were level with the man's knees, and he knew there was no time left, the wave which had carried him so effortlessly up was about to peak, in a last groaning rush he reached the top of the stairs. Now, he thought —and was pitched forward onto the landing with its remaining force, felt the wave shatter around him and the knife jolt out of his sleeve, but he was carried farther than he meant, right past the door down to the end of the landing and up the next flight of stairs in a single unbroken motion, because exactly at this moment the door on the other side of the landing opened and a young woman came out."

Onko fell silent.

"So that was number one," murmured Havel at last, as if to himself. "The dummy run."

"Dummy run?"

"It wasn't the real thing, was it. The real thing was number two. The second attempt."

Havel knocked the ash off his cigar. The man in the hat had told him his views.

"Shall we take a walk?"

And now he would tell him his.

"As you wish."

Everything had fallen into place. Havel blew out the candles, took his coat and followed his guest outside.

They took the elevator and rode down to the street in silence. A cold wind was blowing at the entrance. Havel turned up his collar. They walked to the end of the block, turned right and set off briskly in the direction away from the river. But after a hundred yards Havel unexpectedly stopped, took a bunch of keys out of his pocket and said:

"I think we'll go the rest of the way by car," unlocking the car that stood by the curb and holding the door open. "You may find that you'll have to take off your hat."

Onko got in without a word.

"All set?"

Havel switched on the ignition and swung the car out into the road.

"The dummy run," he resumed, with a glance at Onko. "For it wasn't the real thing, was it. After that first attempt had failed your friend made his way back home. Perhaps *lair* is a better word than home. He must have been in a state of considerable nervous excitement. How else are we to explain what happened when he crawled back into his lair, licking his wounds? Something quite harmless, which nonetheless gave him a very nasty shock indeed."

The car stopped at a traffic light. Onko peered out of the window.

"If it's Long Street we're headed for, don't bother. You needn't run me home."

"As a matter of fact it is Long Street we're headed for," said Havel, "but I'm not running you home."

The light changed and the car surged forward.

"A very nasty shock. For just as he is about to go into his room a door opens on the opposite side of the landing and somebody comes out. He almost jumps out of his skin. Now why's that? He doesn't know that a new tenant has moved in, you see, he thinks the room is still empty. But still, allowing for that, why does the fact of someone coming out of that supposedly empty room at exactly the moment he is unlocking his door give him such a terrific fright? Well . . . your description of the experience he has just got behind him makes it perfectly clear why. I mean, we are talking about the same man, aren't we? For it is raining on the night in question, he is wearing a coat, all these details . . ."

Onko began to tap his knee.

"Here we are . . . amazing how quickly one can get around town at this time of night."

The car slid into Long Street and slowed to a walking pace.

"That night he has a long talk with the new tenant. He already knows about him, as a matter of fact, and during their talk he learns quite a bit more. He stores the information. And a seed is sown. A seed with a marvelous economy of purpose which he will find quite irresistible. . . . He is untroubled by the slightest sense of compunction, you see, in his pursuit of the aesthetic crime. By the time he meets his new acquaintance in a bar a few days later the seed has already burgeoned. He is ready for the second attempt."

Havel accelerated and drove through a red light.

"The real thing was number two. But here I think we can fast-forward, so—"

He flicked a switch and the siren on the roof of the car began to wail. Simultaneously he shifted into second and braked sharply, sending the car into a power slide around the corner, accelerated through another red light and shifted into third. The car swerved to avoid a taxi ahead and thundered down the opposite lane. Havel glanced at the needle, shifted into fourth. The road dipped and entered a tunnel. Lights flared ahead.

"Normally this ride would take about half an hour—"

"There's a car coming."

"There should be room for three . . ."

The lights loomed up and flashed past.

". . . just. But it can be done in ten minutes. Do you drive?"

Onko sat motionless, his hands gripping his knees.

"Are you registered as the owner of a vehicle? Do you vote? What do you do in your spare time?"

The car raced out of the tunnel onto a dual-lane overpass at eighty miles an hour.

"The circumstances of that evening—the evening of the second attempt—make it extremely difficult to establish who was where at what time, how many people actually went to the girl's house and how long they stayed there. In all this confusion it is naturally gratifying to find at least one person whose statement is cast-iron—your friend."

Havel accelerated past a convoy of trucks and cut sharply across into the exit lane.

"He never arrives at the girl's house, he only goes part of the way. He asks the driver of the car to stop. He gets out, and as he is crossing the road nearly manages to get himself run over. This incident is witnessed by a lot of people and he reasons, correctly, that it is the kind of thing they will be likely to remember. His statement is demonstrably true—"

He shifted into third and let the car drift into a banked curve.

"*Demonstratively* true. Considering the murky evidence that is otherwise available this shining documentation has the opposite effect of drawing attention to itself. We feel it is too good to be true. Well . . ."

Havel switched off the siren.

"It isn't true."

The car slowed down and nosed gently into a narrow street. Havel brought it to a halt at a traffic light.

"Are you familiar with this part of town?"

"I don't believe I am."

Their voices sounded much louder.

"Well. From the spot where he gets off . . ."

The lights changed and the car rumbled slowly forward.

". . . which happens to be just about here . . . it's twenty minutes' walk to the girl's house."

"Which girl?"

"The girl who was with them in the bar—didn't I mention that?—her house. Now you will be struck, like myself, by the marked differences between the dummy run and the real thing. At his second attempt your friend seems to have ditched all his principles, the rigmarole of arbitrary numbers, selection on the basis of pure chance, and so on. Naturally I give more weight to the second attempt, for the obvious reason that it succeeded whereas the first did not. After all, what assurance do we have that he would in fact have killed the man whom he followed to that house in the event that someone had not come out onto the landing? Or, for that matter, that anyone did come out onto the landing? Perhaps he just funked. Whereas the second attempt, which is altogether a far riskier affair, where there is an easily established connection between himself, the victim and the circumstances of her death, succeeds against all the odds. This suggests to me that far from being the detached, cool experimenter he represents himself to be he is in fact driven by very powerful, very specific motives—so powerful, indeed, that he goes to the most fantastic lengths to disguise them from himself. It was his intention just to go out and kill a person, as if he were posting a letter, you said, but look at what he actually does when it comes to it. He decapitates a girl and mutilates her corpse. He destroys her in such a manner, he destroys her so utterly, that the fact of his having also—what was the phrase you used?—*terminated a life* becomes almost incidental."

Havel swung the car off the main road, cut the engine and coasted to a standstill at the end of a little street.

"I think we have arrived," he said softly.

Onko turned and stared at him in silence.

"We shall now reconstruct the events of that night at the place where they happened. Would you like to get out?"

Havel lifted the latch on the gate and took a few steps into the garden. Wind stirred the branches of the bare trees which in the brilliant moonlight cast moving shadows across the frosted lawn. Above him the house towered, with shuttered windows, in darkness and utter silence. He sensed Onko behind him. For a minute neither of them spoke. They watched and listened.

"There!" said Havel suddenly.

He raised his arm and pointed.

"That's where he saw her. At the top window. He was waiting here in the garden. He must have felt it like a summons. He never followed the others around the back of the house to the basement. He saw her and went straight up. —What d'you think? —Through the front door. Just like that."

He bounded up the steps, turned the handle and pushed the door.

"Open, you see."

Onko stood motionless in the middle of the path.

"How could he have seen her if—?"

"Well exactly!" exclaimed Havel. "How could he? But won't you come up?"

There was a long pause before Onko moved.

Then he put his hands into his pockets, walked briskly up the steps and through the door Havel held open for him into the house. Havel shut the door.

After a few moments Onko said:

"Don't you think your demonstration would benefit if you turned on the lights?"

"Ah. But unfortunately the electricity has been cut off. I have a flashlight, however."

He rummaged in his pockets, and after a moment a beam of light began to grope across the floor.

"Which way from here—do you think?"

"The stairs, if he wanted to go up. How else?"

"Quite! How else? So—"

The light picked out the bottom of the stairs and drifted slowly up.

———

"You go on ahead. I'll light the way from behind."

They began to climb the stairs.

"What feelings does he have?" whispered Havel.

"Feelings?"

"When he starts to go up these stairs. Does that dynamo switch on? Is the blood boiling under his scalp? But can you see your way? Why don't you take hold of the banister?"

"I can see my way."

"Good! And now we arrive—he arrives—at the landing."

Havel's light shone briefly through open doors and illuminated empty rooms.

Suddenly he touched Onko's arm and murmured:

"There's someone coming."

Onko stiffened. There wasn't a sound in the house.

"I hear nothing."

"Oh I don't mean now. I mean he hears someone coming. And that's where he hides."

The light played across the landing until it reached an alcove in the corner under the stairs.

"They took the curtains out with the rest of the furnishings. But there was a curtain there, wasn't there."

"I don't know."

"And that's where he hides, waits. The master of improvisation. And standing there he finds it just slide into his hands—eh?"

"Finds what?"

"The instrument with which he killed her. Puts a hand down and feels the butt of the shaft pressing into his palm. A weapon slides into his hand of its own accord. *Ready to hand.* Boldness pays. He just picks it up, with the same astonishing casualness with which he carries out the whole murder."

Onko turned.

"And then?"

"And then? Well! He waits . . . he has to wait a long time

before they come up. By the look of the boy it's clear that he's not going to be on his feet for much longer. The girl seems to be in better shape. Is she carrying the candle? Is she lighting them to bed? And still he waits—for, what? another five minutes?—to make sure the coast is clear. Then he goes up."

Havel turned the flashlight to the stairs and began to walk up.

"Like this."

Onko followed. Havel paused at the edge of the upper landing and waited until Onko was standing beside him.

"As far as here. And suddenly there's no more time. The girl has stepped out of her gown and comes out of the room—there!—naked, just as he reaches the top of the stairs. It all happens within seconds. Maybe he hits her from behind, or maybe she sees him and he just hits her so fast that she never utters a sound. He can strike only one blow while she is still standing but it's enough to put her down and perhaps to kill her. The next three or four blows are delivered while she's already lying on the floor—look at her, lying under him on the floor!—and then of course he goes berserk—hacks off her head—horror? fear? no, he feels nothing of that kind. Everything is obliterated in a consuming sexual passion. He drags the body back into the room she came out of alive less than a minute ago. Without the head it is dehumanized, just a carcass, he tosses it onto—what? why *this?*—but his instinct tells him where it belongs—he tosses it onto a jumble of toys and dolls—"

Havel switched off the light.

"And here he performs the final act which—don't you think?—betrays him, here at last—"

"Why have you turned out the light?"

"Because we don't see him. Here at last we get a scent of him, upwind the *smell* of him, the lather of a rank boar sweating in the thickets. He snuffs the burning candle inside her . . ."

Havel paused, and the silence thickened around them.

"Do you catch the smell of him? Ha? Is this the experimenter whose *disinterestedness* you vouched for? Is it the same man?"

"Perhaps not."

Onko's voice came flatly out of the dark.

"Perhaps, perhaps not! Perhaps it was the same man and he changed on his way here . . . for he was worried, wasn't he, from the start, that he was being driven by an erotic sensation of fear. Didn't you say that?"

"Yes."

"Or might you have meant—or might he have been driven by—a fear of erotic sensation? Or even both? What do you think?"

"I think your imagination is overreaching itself."

"My imagination—overreaching itself! From you!" exclaimed Havel.

He waited for a minute in silence, but he knew the moment was irretrievably lost.

"Then perhaps it is time we had the lights on again and went back home."

He turned on the flashlight and followed Onko out of the house.

*T*hey drove back across town in silence, Onko slumped in his seat, beating a tattoo on his knee. Havel felt exhausted. It was half past one. But Onko would not be going to bed yet. He would spend the rest of the night watching the stars from the roof of the warehouse across the river.

He parked the car outside his apartment on the far side of the street.

Onko got out without a word and set off in the direction of the bridge.

Havel began to cross the street, hesitated, turned back.

He found Onko leaning over the parapet of the bridge, looking down at the water. The river's dark icy swirl rushed silently beneath them. The wind had changed. Warmer now, it blew downstream, carrying with it the faint odors of the city.

"But what of his conscience?" asked Havel at last.

"Conscience!"

Onko jerked his head and fell silent.

He seemed to have subsided into a reverie when he added softly:

"Conscience mediates, it is one of three. There, supposedly, it keeps its vigil—out there in the night, hauling offal from a vast reservoir of half-formed, primitive desires; with its back turned, keeping its hands clean and looking east to the always rising light. Is that possible?"

"It's possible."

"But only for someone with the kind of naivety an unmistakable, unmistaking faith can give one. Conscience, as it has to, to endure that otherwise intolerable vigil, reposes in a sense of its own innocence, guaranteed by the certainty that everything behind it is evil, punishably evil. It knows of the things that are behind . . . and it knows of them with dread. But there is also the solace of the light. Almost inaccessible to us now—the language of dread, of solace. It has long since become defunct. For meanwhile the world has changed, and the change is due to knowledge. Knowledge and faith keep uneasy company; proof kills faith stone dead. Conscience is no longer chaste, the notion that it can be impartial no longer tenable. The distinction between Want and Ought has become more subtle, confounded by the assertion that prohibitions originate in desires. Whether this assertion is true or not doesn't matter. It is the spirit of inquiry and the procedure of analysis that matter. This is an absurdly simple procedure: the matter appears to be so, but it is really so. The hat appears to be empty but in reality it contains a warren of white rabbits. The conjurer is hoist by his own petard. The hat appears to be just a hat, but in reality it is another Pandora's box.

"Nothing is as it is. The appearance of things at one with and resting in themselves is merely disingenuous. The surface is subverted by the base; voluntary actions and apparent reasons for which we consider ourselves to be accountable are disqualified by the emergence of hitherto unacknowledged causes, instincts at the base which come rushing out wtih brandished cudgels, base instincts that are involuntary and unaccountable and whose consequences we therefore cannot be accountable for either. Willpower, integrity, self-discipline, restraint, these corrupt and enfeebled custodians of an obsolete spiritual order are bludgeoned and swept aside. Nothing is able to resist the onslaught of the dark autonomous forces, which can only be left to take their course."

He turned on Havel with a snarl.

"And take their course they do—with a vengeance! The incubus strolls out at noon, pays social calls, leaving his card in the most respectable houses. The coy posture of conscience, wrapped in seven veils with all its orifices stopped up, begins to look ridiculous. It is stripped naked and summarily uncorked, revealing a Janus-headed beast with a passage as broad as daylight, broad enough to accommodate not only all the old, covert desires but desires half understood or quite unknown, the multiple intromission of sons and fathers into mothers and daughters, anything admissible in the name of the monster that masquerades as liberated humanity, and a lot that is inadmissible too, murderous, bestial desires, unforgettable and unforgivable. The carnival becomes a purgatory. The new inquisitors, hunters who come soft-footed at daybreak from waiting cars, knocking on marked doors with their casual, petrific mace; the branding of other heretics, in their hundreds of thousands, the immolation of many more, of millions, sticks of men and women, melting like scorched candles. Casual. Crimes of dispassion. Crimes committed as a pastime. The criminals can be punished and their doctrines execrated, but you cannot extirpate the roots of this unfeeling, a mass insensibility, a terrible numbness of the human spirit. It is beyond retrieval, a new high-water mark, a new measure of catastrophe to which we have long since adjusted. Nothing imaginable can be worse than what already was. We are all pragmatists now. The fundamental questions have become questions of mere expediency."

"What you say is unacceptable . . ."

Havel rested his head in his hands.

". . . and would remain unacceptable even if it were true for yourself. But I'm not going to discuss these things with you. I want an answer to one—"

Onko cut him short.

"Then why don't you ask him that question yourself? He was with me in the bar that night. He went to the party at the girl's house. And perhaps he killed her. My friend. You should ask him."

Havel looked at him astounded.

"Or has all this been for my benefit? Do you want an answer from me? Would you believe it?"

"Perhaps I would."

"I did not kill the girl. I had nothing to do with her death. You have been poking your nose into my life. I do not like that. And you have come up with a plausible explanation. If I was you I might believe what you believe, knowing all that you do. But your explanation is wrong. I did not kill the girl."

"And if you did? What would you say in that case? Would you admit it?"

"Naturally I would deny it."

Havel was utterly nonplussed.

Onko turned and walked away across the bridge.

———

Certain peculiarities that had been evident in the defendant's manner from the beginning of the trial became more pronounced the longer it continued. Often he sat with legs crossed and arms folded, his head turned to one side, as if he lacked any interest in or were deliberately ignoring the court proceedings; and at times he clasped his hands over his head, concealing his face behind his arms. Some observers construed this behavior as apathy or resignation, others as frustration, perhaps shame. But then he began to startle the court with intermittent chuckles and unintelligible exclamations. Frequently the judge called the defendant to order and on one occasion, when these interruptions persisted, even found it necessary to have him removed from court.

His performance in the witness box was characterized by similar irregularities. He showed extreme reluctance when called to the witness box and then, when asked to stand down, the same reluctance to leave it. Guided cautiously by the defense counsel, who phrased all his questions in the third person, he gave coherent answers, but when subjected to the blunt interrogation of the prosecution he completely lost his composure. Increasingly, instead of giving answers, he challenged the prosecutor with counterquestions; some of them were remarkably astute, but more of them, like his answers, failed to make any sense at all. And here the tremendous strain of the trial upon its protagonist became daily more apparent; in the rapid deterioration of the defendant's mind, and most particularly in his incompatibility with the surroundings of his trial, in the disturbing impression that Thomas N. and the court were engaged with two entirely distinct inquiries.

At the end of the second week the defendant was asked if there was anything further he wished to say to the court. He scribbled a note which was read out by the defense counsel: the defendant wished only to hear the verdict.

On the following Monday the judge commenced his summing up.

The divergence of the arguments put forward by the prosecution and the defense respectively, he said, reflected the inherent ambiguity of the case on which they turned. While the defense supplied interpretations of events rather than accounts of events, and had accordingly sought to sustain a theory of coincidences, the prosecution had urged the court to take everything at face value, to accept that everything was exactly as it appeared to be, even in those aspects of the evidence, notably the evidence of the defendant himself, where it was difficult to discern any face values at all.

The case for the defense rested on an endeavor to explain *why* the defendant had behaved as he had. Although such explanations were admissible and relevant, they should not distract the jury from the question *if* he had done the crime with which he was charged. The case for the prosecution depended upon circumstantial evidence that the defendant was guilty of the murder of Nancy Fleming. The members of the jury would have to decide whether that evidence, on the grounds of certainty rather than feasibility, was sufficient for a conviction. Feasibility alone provided grounds only for an acquittal.

The court was not a court of metaphysical inquiry.

Speculations about the accused, his character and conduct, relating to any matter other than the crime with which he was charged lay beyond the jurisdiction of the court.

In view of the extraordinary nature of the case it was

necessary to impress this fact on the jury with particular emphasis.

The judge then proceeded with his summary of the evidence, and after a recess for lunch completed it in the middle of the afternoon. The members of the jury withdrew to deliberate.

Two days later the court convened to hear their verdict —but they failed to bring in any verdict at all. They had been unable to reach agreement, the foreman said.

In the light of subsequent events, the defendant's reaction to the foreman's announcement took on a special significance. The court was adjourned until the following morning, the public gallery was cleared, and the counsel for the defense withdrew with his client to discuss the implications of the jury's indecision. This discussion never took place, however, for his client was manifestly in a state of such shock that any attempt to talk to him would have been useless. He stood in the corridor white-faced and speechless, "as if he had been sentenced to death," counsel noted; but unfortunately he had to hurry on to a meeting with the public prosecutor in the judge's chambers and could not devote as much attention to his client as in retrospect his condition very clearly warranted. He encouraged him as best he could, gave instructions to a court steward to bring his client a cup of tea and promised to visit him the same evening. That was the last he saw of him.

The court steward testified that the defendant did not drink the tea he had brought him on counsel's instructions. At least he had been able to persuade him to sit down and rest for a few minutes. Shortly afterwards two guards had arrived to escort the defendant back to prison. The steward accompanied them to the back entrance of the court, unlocked and locked the door again behind them, in the course of his normal duties. The defendant had not been handcuffed when he left the building.

Both guards admitted that their prisoner had not been

handcuffed before leaving the court. This omission constituted a breach of regulations—as it turned out, a fatal omission. They had omitted to do so because as they were leaving the building the officer to whom the boy was usually handcuffed noted that one of the shoelaces of the prisoner was undone. For this reason he had not been handcuffed to the prisoner prior to leaving the building. When they got outside he told him to do the shoelace up.

The court building backed out onto a narrow street. The prison van waited at the curb directly outside the entrance. The rear door of the van was open and the driver already waiting in his seat, as was the normal procedure. From the court entrance to the van door it was a distance of only a few yards.

The prisoner did not do up his shoelace. He walked straight on as if with the intention of climbing into the back of the van. The two guards followed immediately behind him, but whether, at the instant he reached the van door, the prisoner tripped, or fell, or dived into the road, they were unable to say with certainty afterwards. The driver of the car was not able to say either, nor any of the surprisingly large number of passersby who happened to be in the locality at the time the incident occurred. Certain only was that shortly after five o'clock in the afternoon Thomas N. was struck and killed instantly by a passing car in the crowded alley directly behind the criminal courts.

Trial proceedings in the case of the murder of Nancy Julia Fleming were thus brought to a close, and the coroner's court which succeeded it with the purpose of clarifying the residual fate of the former defendant of that trial brought in a verdict of accidental death.